Banana Flower

Robert V. Wadden Jr.

ISBN: 978-1-62420-668-9

Credits
Cover Artist: Designs by Ms G
Editor: Sherry Derr-Wille

Chapter One
Palm Beach, Florida

Franklin Dorner felt the warm moist air hit him in the face as he walked out the doors of the air conditioned Carmany bank building on his way to a quick, solitary lunch. Sweat rivulets immediately began to form under his arms beneath the crisp linen suit he wore. Up until recently life had been very good for Dorner. His small private bank was very profitable, now bringing in millions in new deposits. Several lucrative corporate accounts stimulated a growth in staff and resources and a substantial increase in Dorner's salary as CEO and chairman of the board. His sixty percent stock holdings in the bank increased dramatically in value and on paper he was now a multimillionaire. He was able to purchase a large, beautiful new home in the Flamingo Park neighborhood. He now drove a new Bentley Mulsanne.

All this prosperity came with a price. The new corporate accounts were controlled by a group of Colombians who used them, and Carmany bank, to launder money. Dorner told himself he had no knowledge of the origins of the funds which poured into his bank, some by wire from Panamanian banks and some in cash unloaded in unmarked boxes from unmarked trucks on random occasions. He had not shown any curiosity about the origins of this money and also not reported the cash deposits, which amounted to millions of dollars, to the Internal Revenue Service as required by the Federal Bank Secrecy Act. For two years that had not been a problem until somehow an IRS agent, bank auditor and FBI agent showed up at the bank with a very good idea of what they were looking for.

Dorner walked into a little Cuban café two blocks from the bank building and slid into a seat at a table. He ordered a Cuban sandwich and iced coffee. While he waited for his order, he thought about the deal he cut with the federal agents. He agreed to cooperate fully with their investigation. In return while the bank would pay a three and one half million dollar fine, it would not be closed down. He would not be charged with any crimes. The fine and, more importantly, the loss of the Colombian business, would be devastating to the bank. Their deposits would likely be impounded and he would have to start from scratch to develop new business. The Bentley and maybe the Flamingo Park house would have to go. But Dorner was an optimist and he knew he had been lucky to escape prison. The FBI offered to put him and his family into witness protection. "The Colombian's are dangerous," Agent Hornsby told him. "It's important to them to send a message. They would have expected you to go to jail rather than cooperate."

Dorner felt that had been an attempt to scare him. The Feds did not want him to continue in banking and relished the idea of him pumping gas in some hick town in Indiana or Arizona. He had just been a go between for the Colombians not a coconspirator or partner in crime. He felt he had little to give the feds. The Colombians were aware of that and would feel no need to send any kind of message.

Besides, the one Colombian with whom he had contact, Alejandro Ortega, was a gentlemanly, civilized soul. Alejandro with his five-thousand-dollar Rolex and European tailored Italian suits and his talk of Federico Garcia Lorca and Jorge Luis Borges was not the sort you would associate with violence. A trim six feet tall with a slender mustache and graying temples, Alejandro immediately charmed him and put him at ease. It was like dealing with an erudite college professor rather than a representative of a Medellin cartel. Alejandro presented the arrangement as a business opportunity. His people had large amounts of profit they needed to invest in the United States. Franklin's bank needed deposits, preferably large ones. Had Alejandro been some jumped up gangster in a cheap suit with a scarred face and bad manners Dorner would have had serious hesitation about getting involved. An elegant, literate gentleman with refined manners left Franklin thinking he was dealing with someone he could trust.

When he got back to his office at the bank, Dorner got a call from Alejandro. "Franklin, my friend, how are you?" said the soft, slightly accented voice on the other end. "My sources tell me you have been contacted by federal agents who may be investigating our little arrangement."

"So far I've told them nothing, not a thing," Dorner said, omitting the fact that he had, in fact, agreed to tell them everything.

"May I suggest you get yourself a lawyer, a very good lawyer, I can recommend several then tell them nothing. It will be best for all of us if you reveal nothing of our arrangements."

"What do you mean 'best for all of us'?"

"You do not want to go to jail do you? My associates would not want the details of their financial arrangements to become known. They could confiscate all of our money and put your bank out of business. I would not recommend your federal penal institutions for a man of your stature. It could be quite brutal. A good lawyer will help you fight them and at least delay problems while other arrangements can be made."

"Well, they know something already, that's how they got on to us in the first place. Someone in the bank or on your side has given them information. They already know about the cash shipments."

"I am sorry to hear that but it does not change the strategy. Delay them as long as possible while we destroy records and move our funds elsewhere."

Dorner did not mention that as they spoke bank examiners were reviewing his records and a court order had been issued freezing funds in the bank. It was only a matter of time before the shell corporations whose accounts were frozen would receive formal notice.

"It may be too late to move the funds. They are already on top of that. I told you they came to me already knowing about the cash. Somebody leaked information and it wasn't me or any of my people."

"Of course not, Franklin. For you to tell them anything would be a ticket to prison for you. You were doing well with our arrangement. So, it wouldn't be you. For now, please, tell them nothing, even if they offer you a deal. Don't trust them. I'll talk to my principals and see what they wish to do. Perhaps we will have no choice but to write off the amounts we have in Carmany Bank and find another place to do business. You understand, do you not?"

"Yes, of course. You would leave me holding the bag?"

"Sadly, there is little we can do for you now. As I said I can recommend an excellent lawyer to help who perhaps can keep you out of jail, but the financial damage is inevitable, for both of us. Franklin, I will miss our little talks it has been a pleasure doing business with you. I am sorry it had to end this way, but I feel we will both land on our feet when this is over. Goodbye."

Jail was no longer a possibility. The deal with the feds had been made. Franklin wondered what they would do to Alejandro. He felt bad because he liked the man. In reality, survival trumped friendship and it had come to that.

Chapter Two
Spackenkill Hamlet, New York State

The VanDerlies house sat on an acre and a half of untended grounds overgrown with weeds, gnarled century old apple trees as well as dead rose bushes. The house itself, built in the eighteen-eighties, was a Victorian monstrosity of dark stone, turreted towers and arched windows. The house was in even worse disrepair than the surrounding grounds. There were roof shingles missing, gutters hanging askew, mold on the dark stone exterior, peeling paint on the doors and window frames.

The VanDerlies family came to North America in the seventeenth century when New York City was known as "New Amsterdam" and New York was a Dutch colony. For years the family prospered, owning hundreds of valuable acres in the rich Hudson Valley. The present decaying mansion was on the last plot of that land which had been sold off for years to maintain the family's lifestyle long after their fortunes declined.

The present occupant of the house was Eric VanDerlies. He was the last remaining male member of the family. An undergraduate at Harvard, he took his law degree at Yale. Now at fifty-five he was retired and lived alone. His entire career had been spent in the FBI. While he was known as a brilliant agent, he never achieved any leadership role and retired as a senior agent. Colleagues found him prickly, arrogant and difficult to deal with. He quickly developed a reputation as someone who was not a team player. He survived because he could be highly effective at complex investigations. Much of his career had been spent in counter-espionage. He also spent time working on high profile cases involving financial crimes and homicides. He made few friends in the agency and was routinely passed over for promotion.

When Chandler Diaz, a black Cuban American, was named to head the special high profile homicide team Eric thought he should lead, he decided to retire. Diaz was everything VanDerlies was not. The son of an immigrant father and a black hotel maid, he graduated from a state college, then a mediocre law school then clawed his way into favor by groveling to his superiors. Eric saw himself as a 'real' American whose ancestors fought in the Revolution and Mexican American war, served as officers in the Union Army and in the New York State legislature. He had pedigree and went to the best schools. Yet in the FBI he was constantly shunted from unit to unit, clashing with his supervisors and detested by his fellow agents. The Diaz promotion was the last straw.

He now spent quiet days working on Greek and Latin translations of classic works. Currently, he was working on an obscure play by Aeschylus, the father of Greek tragedy, one he believed had not previously been translated. He had obtained a copy of an original manuscript from a friend at the Metropolitan Museum of Art. Between his retirement and the frugal remains of the family fortune, he had enough to live on, though not nearly enough to keep up the house and grounds.

As he sat in his study working on translating a particularly complex sentence, his cell phone rang. He recognized the number and debated on whether to answer. A call from Assistant FBI Director Patricia Patterson was not likely to be good news. Against his better judgement he answered.

"Eric, how are you?" the Assistant Director's voice was dry and emotionless. It was quite clear she did not give a damn how he was.

"I'm enjoying retirement. I suspect that's not what you called to find out."

"I'll cut right to the chase and skip the rest of the pleasantries. I'm planning to be in New York City on Friday and I'd like to meet with you."

"I can't imagine why you would want to do that. I'm retired and you were never a fan."

"True, but we need your help. Something very bad has happened and we need someone to take a fresh look at the problem."

"May I know what it is you want my help with?"

"I'll tell you when we meet on Friday. It's not a long drive and, of course, you can always say no."

"Would I be paid for this 'fresh look'?"

"Yes, if you decide to take it on, we'll hire you as a consultant and pay your expenses."

"What time are we meeting?"

Chapter Three
Palm Beach, Florida

Every Saturday Franklin Dorner played golf at the Emerald Dunes Club. It was his relaxation time away from his wife and two daughters. It was also a chance to develop business, work on relationships with potential bank clients and those who might refer clients. This Saturday his party included Jason Bart, the owner of a three-restaurant group and Andrew Kasey, a financial advisor based in Palm Beach. Dorner made sure there was a chilled thermos of dry martinis and clear plastic cups for breaks between holes.

Bart was the best golfer of the three, possibly because his business was well established and he had more time on the links than Dorner or Kasey. By hole seven he was several strokes ahead. At that point Dorner decided it was time for a cocktail break. They pulled their carts into a palmetto grove. Dorner poured drinks and pulled out Chex Mix to provide a salty accompaniment to the martinis. The seventh was on the edge of the course with a buffer of palmetto trees screening it from a nearby road.

As they stood under the trees laughing and drinking, a young woman stepped out of the inner grove. She was dressed in a beige linen blouse, with a light blue silk scarf, tight faded jeans and open toed sandals. Tall, blonde and shapely with huge blue eyes the woman was astonishingly lovely. Obviously, she was not a golfer.

"I'm so sorry," she said "my car broke down and my cell phone battery is dead, I thought I might find someone on the course who could help."

"Sweetheart," said Kasey, "what can we do to help?"

"If I could just use one of your cell phones to call Triple A that would be perfect," she said smiling at them.

"How could we refuse such a pretty girl?" said Bart reaching into his pocket for his phone.

"Let me just pull out my Triple A card, the number is right on the back."

When she pulled her hand out of her purse it held a black pistol with a thick cylinder on the muzzle. They heard a pop and Dorner went down with a red hole in his forehead and a larger hole in the back of his head. Brain matter spattered Kasey who had been standing next to him. The next shot hit him in the chest and he fell immediately. Bart took off running and yelling. He collapsed with a shot that hit him in the back of the knee. As he lay there moaning in agony the pretty girl stood over him with the pistol pointed at his head.

"Hard to outrun a bullet," she said and squeezed off a round that hit him square in the forehead.

There was no one else around the seventh hole to see the commotion and the vague popping sound of the pistol could not have carried very far. The girl put the pistol back in her purse and walked over to Dorner's corpse looking down. "Sorry to have made such a mess but the Colombians like to send a message." She looked around to make sure she left no footprints then slipped back into the palmetto grove, climbed the fence, hopped into a car parked by the side of the road and drove away.

Chapter Four
FBI Regional Headquarters, Federal Square, Manhattan

VanDerlies had been in the Javits Federal building numerous times. He even worked there for nine months on an assignment until his supervisor asked to have him transferred. When he got to the FBI offices he was ushered into an outer office and told to wait. It was at least twenty minutes before they walked him into a large, bare office. Behind the wide, empty desk sat a middle-aged woman with graying blonde hair, a lined, weary face and faded blue eyes. She was stockier than he remembered her. "Assistant Director," he greeted her.

She nodded and indicated for him to sit on one of the chrome framed leather chairs in front of the desk. For some reason he felt like a pupil summoned before the principal for misbehavior. He had to remind himself he no longer worked for the Agency.

"Have you kept up on Agency gossip since you've been gone?"

"Not really."

"You won't have heard that Chandler Diaz was murdered."

"No, I can't say that I have. Couldn't happen to a nicer fellow though."

"I know you never liked Diaz, but that's no reason to celebrate his death. He was a good agent and a decent man. What's most important he was one of ours. When an agent is killed, the Agency has to take action."

"Okay, what does that have to do with me?"

"Diaz was killed in a Manhattan hotel room. Shot through the forehead with an eight-millimeter. He had just conducted an operation that ended in abject failure. We think there is a connection but so far, we have absolutely nothing on the killer. Our best people have come up with a complete blank. You may not have been the most popular agent in FBI history, you were a piss poor team player, but you were damn good working on your own, one of the best at putting together complex puzzles

I've ever seen. We need your help to find Diaz' killer."

"What's in it for me?"

"You mean besides the satisfaction of bringing the killer of a fellow FBI agent to justice?"

"Yes, besides all that."

"We'll put you on a retainer, pay all expenses, give you a free hand. Temporarily reinstate your authority as a law enforcement officer. I know you can use the money; besides you must be getting bored translating classical poetry."

"Tell me about the murder."

"Is that a yes?"

"Let's call it a conditional yes. I just need to know a little more about what I am up against."

"Diaz thought he had a line on a serial professional killer, someone who took high profile targets. He set up a sting using an e-mail he found from a former client who hired the killer. The killer was meant to think that the intended target was an Argentinian diplomat. We used an agent to impersonate the fictitious diplomat who was supposed to be visiting the U.N. in New York. The Agency fronted one hundred thousand dollars to the killer after we took a contract out using an e-mail we got from a suspect involved in an earlier killing."

"Did you try to trace the e-mail?"

"Of course. It was with a Russian service company, but it was routed through servers all over the world. Could have originated anywhere. Ultimately, there was no attempt on the undercover target who was under constant surveillance."

"So, it was Diaz who ended up dying?"

"The night we shut down the operation everyone went home. Diaz was staying in a midtown Manhattan hotel. He stopped for a drink in the hotel bar. The bartender remembered him talking to a blonde woman. She even bought him a drink."

"Did she…?"

"She paid cash."

"Did we get a description?"

"Blonde, about five seven, pale skin, large blue eyes, maybe late twenties. The security cameras in the lobby and elevator show Diaz leaving with a blonde but she never gave the camera a good angle to show a very clear view of her face."

"Was she a prostitute?"

"Bartender says no, and he should know. He said she was too well dressed to be a hooker and just didn't give off that vibe. She did approach Diaz, though, the bartender remembers that. We couldn't find anyone else in the bar that night who remembered her."

"Was there any evidence to indicate the professional killer they were looking for in the failed operation was a woman?"

"No. I think they made the assumption it was a male. Most pros are male. There was nothing specific to lead them in either direction."

"Forensic evidence?"

"The hotel room was very clean. Diaz had gotten a bottle of Irish whiskey out with two glasses. He was killed with a single shot through the forehead. He died instantly. No one heard a shot. No one saw anyone leave the room. Ballistics couldn't match the bullet to any known weapon and we never did find the murder weapon."

"Sounds like a pro, a good one, but why?"

"We're not sure. Diaz' trap may have failed, but perhaps he was on to something, someone didn't want him to get any further. At this point it's all speculation."

"Do we think the girl did it?"

"She could have, or she could have been a lure to set him up for the killer. Well, are you interested?"

"I am. As you well know, I can use the money. I do find this to be an interesting case. It takes real audacity to murder an agent. Whoever did it had to know we would come after them. Do I get to work alone on this?"

"I don't think I could find anybody who would be willing to partner with you, so yes you are on your own. I do want you to connect with the NYPD homicide detective who not only investigated Diaz' murder but worked with him on some of the earlier homicides that Diaz was convinced were done by the killer he tried to trap. She can provide you with some background."

"She?"

"I know you have a reputation for disapproving of female law enforcement officers. You certainly seemed to resent me in the time you worked under my supervision. Despite your misgivings, this is a very competent detective. Diaz trusted her and she was very upset when his body was found. Since there seems to be a connection between his murder and the suspect in the earlier murders, she and Diaz worked on together she'll provide some deep background that may be helpful. Her name is Becky Haden and I'll see if I can set up a meeting for you this afternoon while you're in town."

Chapter Five
New York City, NYPD Headquarters, 1 Police Plaza

The guy who walked into her cubicle was skinny, maybe fifty years old with salt and pepper hair cut short, clean shaven with a sharp, jutting jaw and deep-set brown eyes. He also looked like he had a poker shoved up his ass. He was wearing khakis, a white shirt open at the collar and a blue blazer.

"Eric VanDerlies," he said offering his hand.

Assistant Director Patterson warned her about this guy. He was a really good agent, smart, very eccentric. He did not like people of color and wasn't wild about women law enforcement officers. He retired when Diaz moved past him for a promotion and lived alone. Patterson rehired him to work on the Diaz case because they were getting nowhere. Haden knew she didn't look much like the stereotype of a police officer, certainly not a detective. This VanDerlies guy was seeing a pert, five foot, six-inch-tall woman still in her late twenties with blonde hair cut in a cute bob. She knew some of the men in homicide called her 'detective Barbie' behind her back and suspected that is exactly what VanDerlies saw when he looked at her.

"Becky Haden," she answered taking his hand in a limp, insincere handshake. "Have a seat. I understand you want to talk about Chandler Diaz' murder."

"That's right."

"What do you need to know?"

"Diaz was caught on camera with a woman he apparently met in his hotel bar. Was she ever seen leaving the hotel?"

"No, we went through hours of security camera footage and never saw her after she went up in the elevator with Agent Diaz."

"Any witnesses besides the bartender? Maybe someone in the lobby or a hallway?"

"No one we could find."

"You worked with Diaz on this serial professional killer thing. What made you think the various murders were connected?"

"They were linked to Cayman Islands bank accounts which were all linked to the same Panamanian corporation. The clients wired money to the islands and it was funneled through the same corporation which was owned by a trust. We had inside information that the trust beneficiary was a woman named Maria Guisado."

"A woman?"

"Yes, we couldn't find anything about her other than some immigration records that showed her leaving the U.S. and entering Panama. We assumed it was a pseudonym that was just used on a passport. We thought she might be part of an organization that trafficked in professional hits."

"Why an organization?"

"Well, we linked the Panama corporation to nine different killings in less than a year, including some in Singapore. That's a lot of work for a single killer."

"But not impossible."

"No, not impossible. We never ruled anything out."

"Do you think this mysterious woman who picked up Diaz in a bar could have been Maria Guisado?"

"Sure, assuming Maria Guisado actually exists. She could have been anybody. She wasn't necessarily the murderer."

"Do you think there was a connection between Diaz' attempted 'sting' and his murder?"

"We have no hard evidence to suggest that but somehow it seems unlikely it was a coincidence. We know of no one else who had a strong motive to murder Diaz. My gut feeling is that there is a connection."

"What happened to the Panama corporation?"

"It dissolved and the owners stopped using the Panama City law firm where we had an informer. The Cayman accounts were all closed."

"So, all those threads to the murderer are useless now?"

"Pretty much."

"Can we look at the security camera footage?"

15

Haden took him down several floors to a room lined with computer monitors. She took a seat in front of one and pulled out a keyboard. She rattled off a sequence of keystrokes and a grainy image came up on the monitor. The first image to appear on the screen was of a blonde woman walking through the hotel lobby dressed in a black, sleeveless dress belted at the waist and hemmed above the knee. She appeared to be about five foot seven inches tall if you discounted the patent leather stiletto heels, she wore. Her face was turned away from the camera but was visible in profile. "Looks like she was aware of the placement of the cameras. Her turning away from the cameras looks deliberate."

The next image showed the same woman walking arm in arm with a tall light skinned Black man in a grey suit. The man appeared a bit wobbly suggesting he may have had too much to drink. Again, the woman averted her face from the security cameras.

"You're right, she is clearly aware of the cameras," said Haden.

"I wonder if she did surveillance on the lobby before setting up the encounter with Diaz?"

"We went back a few days on the security footage and didn't see anyone who looked like her."

"Maybe you were looking for the wrong person? Maybe she was in disguise when she cased the place? Maybe she was in disguise when she met Diaz?"

"Or in disguise both times?"

"Can we go back and look at the old security tapes for the lobby? I'm assuming there are no other cameras in the hotel that could have caught her?"

"The lobby is the only place covered by security cameras. We have footage going back a month before the murder but we've already gone over them. I'm not sure what you expect to find."

"Maybe nothing but it's a place to start. There always has to be a place to start."

Chapter Six
Sainte-Marie, Island of Guadeloupe

Amelie looked in on her mother in the only bedroom in their cement block home. She was still asleep on the metal frame bed snoring lightly. At nineteen Amelie was the sole support for her mother and herself. For the last two years she worked in a little restaurant in the town of Goyave waiting tables. As the local economy faltered business at the restaurant fell off and the proprietor reluctantly had to let her go. Although young she was a hard worker and smart. She spoke French and English in addition to her native Creole. He told her about an American woman who had purchased the old Villa Dupleve. She was looking for a housemaid, preferably one who spoke English. Amelie was on her way to interview for the job.

The bus ride was a little over a half hour. She got off at the intersection of the highway and a dirt road which ran among groves of banana trees. She trudged down the road for nearly a quarter mile when the road split. She turned right, toward the coast and walked a narrow lane continuing through banana groves. A man working in the grove by the road called to her in creole. "Where you goin' little honey?"

"I'm going to see the mademoiselle in the Villa Dupleve."

"It's just up the road a bit but the mademoiselle is not in, you'll find her on the beach. Just follow the walkway to the right of the villa and go on down toward the sea, you'll find her."

Amelie wondered how this worker knew the whereabouts of the villa's mistress. She thanked him and continued down the road.

Sheltered from the lane by palm trees, heliconia, hibiscus and bougainvillea the old villa had recently received a fresh coat of paint, coral pink with white shutters on its tall windows with arched transoms. A porch ran the length of each of its two stories which were topped by a high peaked red tile roof. The upstairs porch was lined with French windows also topped by arched transoms and enclosed with white shutters. An old Land Rover was parked by the side of the lane next to the house. As the workman told her, a brick path ran toward the far end of the villa. She followed it and found herself on a stone terrace in the back of the house. A series of stairs led down through terraced planters filled with red bougainvillea toward a line of coconut palms below. Beyond the coconut palms was a white sandy beach. Amelie could make out a chaise longue and a reclining figure on the beach.

As she descended the stairs, she was assailed by the salt smell of the ocean. Beyond the palms a woman with long dark hair lay topless on the chaise. Her pale skin was adorned only with a thong bikini bottom. On a small table beside her was an ice bucket with a bottle of champagne and a glass flute half full of straw-colored liquid.

"Who's there?" the woman asked as Amelie approached her from behind.

"*Mademoiselle*, my name is Amelie, sent by Henri at La Conque."

As the woman turned toward her, Amelie was dazzled by her beauty. Despite lying in the sun her skin was a delicate white, her uncovered breasts were firm and shapely. She had long elegant legs with just a hint of defined muscle. It was her face that was most lovely; subtly defined cheekbones, lush lips and huge blue eyes of a delicate pale shade. Around her neck was a silver chain with a single blue stone that matched her eyes.

"Oh yes. He said he knew someone who might be a good housekeeper. You used to work for him, didn't you?"

"*Oui, Mademoiselle* until business fell off and he could not afford to keep me."

"You speak English, that's very good. I don't speak Creole at all and I'm just learning French. Do you speak French?"

"*Oui*, I mean yes, *Mademoiselle*, I am fluent although we speak Creole at home."

"You can call me Ariella, that's my name. Let me tell you about the job. I expect you to be here five days a week, from nine to four-thirty. Does that work with your bus schedule?"

"Yes, *mademoiselle*, I mean Ariella. I live with my mother in

Sainte-Marie. The bus runs every hour, it should work."

"I'll expect you to clean and pick up. Do you cook?"

"Nothing fancy, but yes, I can cook local dishes. Sometimes I worked in the kitchen at La Conque. So, you want me to cook?"

"I'm not much good in the kitchen and Goyave is a bit far to go out to eat every day, so I'd like you to prepare things I can heat up after you've left. Will that work?"

"I think so, yes. May I ask who else lives in the villa?"

"No one else, just me."

Amelie marveled to think this huge house was just for one person to live in. "The other thing is that I will not be here all the time. I have a house in California and I travel a lot, for business. When I'm not here, I still want you to come to keep the house tidy. The pay is four hundred Euros a week."

Amelie was startled. This was more money than she ever earned. It was an excellent salary for the island, more than she could have hoped to make doing anything else.

"Are you married, Amelie? Do you have a boyfriend?"

"No, I have no time. I work and take care of my mother, who is ill. There is no one."

"How sad, you are a very pretty little thing. You must have your share of admirers?"

In truth there were several men who sought her attentions. She had little time for them and even less interest.

"I suppose, *mademoiselle,* I mean Ariella. A woman so beautiful as you must have a husband or a lover or both?"

As soon as she said this Amelie worried she had been too forward but the woman only laughed.

"Well, I had a boyfriend but he died."

"Oh, I am so sorry. Was this recently? How did he die?"

"Very recently and he was shot," said the woman with a curious smile. "Why don't I take you up and show you the house? I feel as if you will be perfect for the job."

She put on a sheer white cover-up which actually covered up very little as her breasts were clearly visible through the material. Amelie reflected that no island woman would have shown off her body so brazenly as this white woman.

Amelie had been by the Villa Dupleve a few times. It was built around the beginning of the twentieth century by a French planter who owned over one hundred acres of the surrounding property. He was among the first on the island to cultivate bananas for export. The family died out years ago and the villa had been unoccupied for almost a decade. Amelie remembered it as more of a ruin than a place fit for habitation, with broken windows, peeling paint, shutters falling apart, cracks in the walls and loose tiles on the roof. The grounds had been overgrown and littered.

Clearly the place had been renovated. The bougainvillea in the planters was neatly trimmed and the stairs intact. The terrace at the rear of the house had new outdoor furniture, a large glass and metal table and chairs, several more chaise lounges. Ariella opened the French doors into the villa. They walked into a large room with a stone floor, Amelie thought some kind of marble, with strikingly modern furniture. There was a long, lime green couch, several sleek mahogany side tables as well as a glass and metal coffee table. On the far wall was a mahogany bar well stocked with bottles of liquor and clean glasses.

They passed through this room into a formal living room with a large couch and matching chairs. To the left was a solid mahogany door. "It's always locked," said Ariella, "it's my private office and you are to stay out of it under all circumstances."

They passed into a large library with mostly empty shelves lining the room and a long hardwood table in the middle. "Keep this room well dusted. If there are books or papers on the table, do not move them or put them away. Just leave them where you find them."

They turned around and went back through the living room into a large dining room with a mahogany trestle table and a matching sideboard. From there they went through swinging double doors into a butler's pantry and a large kitchen. The kitchen was equipped with stainless steel appliances including an eight-burner propane stove with a griddle and a double door refrigerator. The floor was black and white tile and the walls of the entire room were tiled in white subway tile. "You will find this very well equipped. Do you drive?"

"No, Ariella. We've never had a car."

"Well, when I'm here I can drive you into Goyave to shop."

"I know of a fisherman who could deliver fresh fish to you as well as someone to bring fruit and vegetables to the house."

"Excellent, that may save us a few trips. Upstairs are bedrooms. The only one you need to worry about is mine. The others may just need to be dusted every once in a while."

"Will you ever be having guests?"

"Highly unlikely. I have no friends and no family. As I mentioned, my lover is dead, so I live a very solitary life which is exactly how I prefer it. When can you start, Amelie? I expect to be traveling next week so I'd like you to be able to start right away to settle in before I leave."

Chapter Seven
Redondo Beach, California

Lindsay sat in the drab waiting room of the drab FBI branch office in a drab office building feeling anxious and annoyed. The Hermosa police finally referred her to the local FBI office regarding her complaints about the disappearance of her friend, Fred Cornwall. No trace of him had been found. Meanwhile, the bank was foreclosing on his condominium and his car had been repossessed. After what seemed to Lindsay to be a cursory investigation Hermosa police, referred the investigation to the FBI.

After a half hour wait, she was walked back to the office of a Daniel Holmgren. The office, like the waiting room, was drab and boring. Holmgren, a thirty-something man with a short haircut, a cheap khaki suit and pale blue tie, sat behind a gray metal desk. On one side of the room a gray metal bookcase contained a few thick binders. On the other side of the room was a gray metal filing cabinet. The window behind Holmgren was framed by dusty metal blinds. On his desk was a blotter, a brown plastic pen holder, a telephone and nothing else.

"So, you reported a Fred Cornwall, a local lawyer, as missing about nine months ago and so far, Hermosa P.D. hasn't found a trace of him. Is that right?"

"Yeah, pretty much."

"Hermosa sent over their file. None of Cornwall's business associates, friends, clients have seen or heard from him since you reported him missing. His bank account and credit cards are unused and none of his bills have been paid. We've run a trace on him and haven't found that he has left the country or traveled as far as we can see. He did make a trip to Panama a few months back, but that was long before you reported him missing."

"Yeah, I saw him after he got back from that trip. He took it with that girl."

"Yes," said Holmgren looking up, "that's where it gets interesting. You say he was involved with a woman named Ariella Blumkin?"

"Yes, that's who he took the trip to Panama with and he was dating her."

"No one seems to be able to trace this woman since she graduated from UCLA. It's as if she were dead."

"No, she's not. I saw her."

"Well, we can't find an address for her, her social security number has been dormant for years, she doesn't seem to work anywhere, has no driver's license, hasn't ever filed a tax return, all we know about her is that she graduated *magna cum laude* from UCLA seven years ago and hasn't been seen or heard from since."

"I saw her. She was picking up Fred in a gray Camry in front of his place."

"We can't find any vehicles registered in her name, not a gray Camry or anything else. You never had a license plate number on that car, right?"

"Right, I mean I never thought it would be important and anyway it all happened so fast. I was just, you know, passing by."

"Okay. Let's assume for a moment that you are right and you did see Ariella Blumkin picking up your friend. What makes you think she might have had anything to do with his disappearance?"

"Because she was a psycho, weird and mean. She beat some girl up for teasing her. Her mom, brother and grandfather were murdered. She didn't shed a single tear. Besides, she was too pretty for Fred, totally out of his league, something had to be up."

"None of these things give us a good reason to think she would hurt Fred."

"I know it, I know she did."

"Maybe they just ran off together, eloped, went back to Panama?"

"You just said there was no record of him leaving the country. There would be wouldn't there? Besides, why would he leave everything; his job, his home, his car? Wouldn't he have cleaned out his bank accounts or be using his credit cards?"

"You're right, if he took off someplace there would be some sort of trace. That still doesn't implicate this Ariella girl and doesn't prove she still exists. Do you have a picture of her?"

"No. Wait, I do, I have her yearbook picture. She was a senior when I was a freshman in high school. I mean it was a long time ago and I'm sure she's different now but it's something, right?"

Chapter Eight
New York City, NYPD Headquarters, 1 Police Plaza

Haden left VanDerlies in the media room after supplying him with hours of surveillance camera footage from the lobby of Diaz' hotel. She had plenty to do and Diaz' murder was an FBI case now. As much as she liked Diaz and wanted to get whoever killed him, she did not find herself liking VanDerlies much. He clearly was skeptical of a female homicide detective and seemed patronizing when he spoke with her. She chuckled to herself to think that the skilled and prolific professional killer in this case might be a woman. She wondered how patronizing he might be toward a woman who murdered nine people and a senior FBI agent. Still, he seemed more than willing to pore over hours of dull footage. He certainly had a work ethic she could respect.

Three hours later he came up to her office with something in hand. "I found her," he said, gloating.

He handed her a grainy print out of a blow up from the surveillance footage. It was a woman dressed in a black and white print dress. She had dark hair pinned back in a bun and wore dark rimmed glasses. Although her face was blurry, she had a small nose and big eyes with elegant cheek bones. "She's quite a looker, isn't she?"

"How do you know it's her?"

"Her build, her bearing, the description we got from the bartender, the little we could see of her in the original surveillance tape. It's her, I'm sure of it."

"So now what?"

"We run her through FBI facial recognition programs using the Agency's files. We might get nothing but it's a place to start, right?"

"Okay, is there anything else we can do?"

"We?"

"I'm in on this. NYPD is in on this. I have authorization to do whatever it takes to assist you on this case. I liked Diaz. I worked with him on the New York cases related to this killer. At least five of these murders were committed within NYPD jurisdiction. So, I'm in."

"I work alone, pretty much always have. Look, you seem like a bright little girl. I'm sure you worked hard on these cases but you are in over your head. That's why they called me in out of retirement. I don't need your help and I don't want a partner."

"I think you do need my help. I was involved in the murders here, I helped Diaz set up his sting, I've studied the financial information we have on the killer."

"So, if you're so clever what would you do next?"

"The one solid connection we have is with Panama. I think I might go to Panama and try to shake some information out of the people who were shepherding our killer's money."

"I'll give you credit, I was thinking something along the same lines."

"We supposedly had an informant inside the law firm that handled the killer's corporation. Maybe that person knows something more. Maybe that informant actually saw our killer?"

"We would need to be careful about treading lightly. Panamanian law protects the confidentiality of these corporations and this law firm is not going to like us trying to get information on one of its clients."

"We?"

"You've got some good ideas, Haden, and you're right. You know more about this case than I do and it helps give me a better head start. I don't like working with a partner, especially not a female partner. So, long as you let me take the lead and defer to my judgement, you're in, at least for now."

"Do you honestly think women are less capable than men at conducting an investigation?"

"No offense, Haden, but women think differently than men. You ride your emotions not your intellect. Besides, doesn't it go without saying that men are stronger and tougher?"

"No. in general women are just as smart and tough as men. I think our instincts are better, especially when it comes to people."

"We'll have to agree to disagree on that. I'll get the name of our inside informant and arrange for two tickets to Panama. We'll leave in two days."

Chapter Nine
Miami Beach, Florida

Alejandro Ortega fingered the fabric of the sports coat on the rack at Massimo Roma, the men's clothiers. It was a fine Italian linen, pale blue and soft to the touch. He loved buying clothes. His closets at home were packed with expensive items and he was always dressed to the nines. The debacle with Carmany bank had been a temporary setback. His funds were somewhat impacted, but he could still afford to buy an eight-hundred-dollar jacket.

He was already working on finding a new set-up for the funds his employers wanted to make available in the U.S. The government impounding the Carmany accounts was unfortunate. He knew someone on the inside of the bank blew the whistle, but he was still not sure who. What happened to Franklin Dorner was even more unfortunate. The man was pleasant enough and he and Ortega had a friendly acquaintanceship. The cartel bosses clearly suspected Dorner of agreeing to cooperate with the Federal investigators. If it was true then Franklin made a big mistake. The one rule in this business was you did not talk or cooperate. He was certain the cartel bosses did not blame him. As he explained, it was just part of the cost of doing business in the U.S.

Things were tighter on the financial side. Even the offshore banks were reporting information back to the Americans. Besides, the cartel wanted the money available in the U.S. for investments, luxury items, operating expenses and the like. The U.S. was, after all, the best place to spend money as he knew all too well. He was now thinking along the lines of a business to use as a front using cartel money as an investment then spiking profits that could be used as ordinary income. So far Medellin had not responded to his proposal.

Ortega was born in Bogota to a family which could trace its heritage to the early days of Spanish settlement. They once owned sugar cane plantations on the Caribbean coast which they farmed with several hundred slaves. Over the years the family sold off their land holdings to finance an increasingly luxuriant lifestyle. By Alejandro's generation, the land and most of the money were gone. There was enough to procure a good education for himself and his siblings though not much more. He used his connections from school to obtain a post in the diplomatic corps eventually being posted to the Colombian consulate in Miami where there was a significant population of Colombian expatriates. It was there he was approached by the cartel to use his connections to set up financial arrangements to launder and invest large sums of cash. His own cut was very generous and he was no longer troubled by trying to live on a diplomat's modest salary. Eventually, he resigned from the consulate and worked full time for the cartel as their Miami fixer. He spoke excellent English, had lots of important contacts and understood how things work in the U.S., something the cartel bosses did not.

He bought the jacket and had his Bentley convertible brought around so he could drive back to his mansion in South Beach. He stopped at a traffic light with his top down enjoying the warm breeze. A small Toyota pulled up next to him. The window on the passenger side rolled down. Ortega saw a blonde woman smile and point a pistol at him. The pistol fired just as the light turned green and the Toyota sped away. Ortega sprawled forward over the steering wheel blaring the Bentley's horn in chorus with the horns of the cars stuck behind him.

Chapter Ten
Panama City, Panama

They put Haden and VanDerlies up in the JW Marriott, a tall tower in the center of the city's high rise commercial district. The rooms were narrow and bland with white tile floors, white walls and plywood and metal furniture. Despite the bland surroundings that could be found in any hotel in any American city, Haden was excited to be out of the country.

She had never traveled outside the United States before. She came from a lower middle-class family whose idea of an exotic vacation was Atlantic City. Her father was a clerk in an accounting firm and her mother was a middle school teacher. She only had two years of community college and, of course, the police academy. She excelled as a patrol woman, moved to Vice. In the Department's effort to bring diversity to traditionally all male divisions she was promoted to detective and assigned to Homicide. Although she was not the first woman in Homicide, she was one of just a handful of female detectives in the division. She faced skepticism, thinly veiled hostility and outright harassment. She held on and gained some respect. Being assigned to work with Diaz on the string of professional hits, including those of a hedge fund executive and his assistant, was a sign that her status in the division had risen. Now, she was the only detective who knew enough about Diaz and his investigation to assist the FBI.

So far what most impressed her about Panama was the heat and humidity. As soon as they stepped out of the airport she was dripping with sweat. Panama City itself surprised her with how modern and big it was with dozens of high-rise buildings giving it a skyline that would have put most American cities to shame. VanDerlies managed to get the contact information for the informant, a clerk at Benedict, Alfaro and Sabredo, the law firm handling the corporation which received money for the murders Diaz was investigating. They had an appointment to talk to her the next day.

Haden wanted to go out into the city to explore but VanDerlies had no interest. He brought materials for the text he was translating and wanted to spend the rest of the day working on it. They agreed they would meet for dinner and work out the questions they planned to ask the next day.

She decided to take a tour of the city. The tour took her by van to the *Casco Viejo,* the seventeenth century old town district with its four plazas, ancient Spanish colonial buildings and narrow, cobblestone streets; the Miraflores locks to view the entry of ships into the canal; a trip down the Amador causeway to view the canal and its islands and a magnificent view of the Panama City skyline. By the time she got back to meet VanDerlies for dinner, it was already dark. She expected him to be angry at her lateness but instead found him at his hotel room desk still working on his translation. He seemed almost surprised to see her.

Although Becky wanted to try a restaurant specializing in local food, VanDerlies insisted on eating in the hotel coffee shop. He was not eager to leave the hotel. He wanted to get to bed early so he would be fresh and alert for their interview with the informant.

The coffee shop, with its pastel wall coverings, stainless steel shelving and storage could have been in any American hotel anywhere in the U.S.

They sat at a faux-granite table in a booth with red vinyl benches. The menu had such exotic fare as chicken club sandwiches, patty melts and chicken fingers. Becky gave up and ordered a cheeseburger with fries. VanDerlies had chicken noodle soup which looked as if it came straight from the can. He was all skin and bones, obviously a light and unimaginative eater.

"So, Eric," she ventured "you've read the files on the various murders Diaz and I investigated. What kind of person do you think our killer is?"

"First of all, I'm not convinced the woman in the hotel bar who picked up Diaz is our killer."

"Why not?"

"Women are rarely professional killers and even more rarely serial killers of any sort. Men are driven by testosterone. We are made to be more aggressive, it's our role in any culture to be warriors and hunters. The murders you and Diaz investigated are brutal but cold. They are carefully planned. I don't see a woman capable of being that brutal and that well organized. Women are emotional. It's why you make lousy accountants and engineers. I see this killer as sociopathic but very controlled. They've harnessed their sociopathy for profit."

"While you're right that female assassins are rare, they are not unknown. I'm thinking of Maria Jimenez, who killed for the Zeta cartel. Idoia Lopez Riano, who killed on behalf of Basque separatists. There was Jeanette Van Nessen who was a high-priced assassin from Holland and Brigitte Mohnhaupt who did assassinations for the Red Army Faction in Germany. I'm sure there are more, but you can't just write off the perpetrator of our murders because of gender bias. Women can be professional killers."

"Those are all exceptions. For every one of them there are hundreds of men who have done the same thing. Our killer could theoretically be a woman but the statistical likelihood is it's a man. Whoever did these killings is violent. Women tend to be less prone to violence than men. It's hormones, testosterone fuels violent behavior"

"What little we know about this one points to a woman."

"What makes you think just one person did all these murders? I tend to think we are dealing with some sort of organization. The degree of organization, the financial arrangements, the sheer volume of killings points to an organization. It's just a lot for one person to accomplish and, please don't be offended, especially for a woman."

He stopped talking for a moment and carefully lifted a spoonful of soup to his mouth.

"Let's just go where the evidence takes us on this and try not to have too many biases. I've found murder is often surprising."

VanDerlies merely grunted in response and continued carefully spooning soup to his mouth. By the time they finished eating it was late and they agreed to meet the next morning for breakfast after which they would take a taxi to meet the informant.

Essie Bruguera was Spanish. She came to Panama during a prolonged recession in Spain in which she lost her job and used up most of her savings. In Panama City she easily found work and made a life for herself. Unmarried in her mid-forties she often felt lonely and unfulfilled. The chance to work for the United States Treasury as an informant was as much about finding some excitement as it was about making extra money. Benedict, Alfaro and Sabredo where she worked as a clerk, specialized in setting up and managing shell corporations used by wealthy clients to shelter large sums of money from the tax authorities of their native countries using the corporate and banking privacy laws of Panama to hide their ownership of large sums of money. However, when the FBI contacted her to ask her to meet with an agent, she was nervous about being seen and insisted it be at an obscure café in the Rio Abajo neighborhood.

Haden and VanDerlies walked into the small, dim Café Ferlito with its dark wooden booths and grey tiled floor. They knew immediately when they saw the plump middle aged, prematurely grey-haired woman sitting alone in a booth that she was who they came to meet. She was dressed in a beige flannel skirt, vertically striped black and white striped sleeveless blouse with her hair in a bun.

"Senorita Bruguera?" said VanDerlies.

She nodded.

"Do you speak English?"

"Of course," said the woman, "please sit down."

"My name is Special Agent Eric VanDerlies from the FBI and this is Detective Haden from the New York Police Department. We just have a few questions and rest assured you'll be compensated for your time."

The woman nodded again but said nothing.

"Are you familiar with a corporation called Medusa, S.A.?"

"Yes, of course. We, the firm, created that corporation for a client."

"Do you know the identity of the client?"

"It was a trust that owned the shares. Under Panamanian law the beneficiary of the trust was confidential."

"You identified that beneficiary to the FBI some time ago did you not?"

"Yes, I filed the trust documents. I noted that the trustee and beneficiary were both a woman named Maria Guisado."

"What can you tell us about this woman?"

"Not too much. I believe she was a Panamanian national with a residence somewhere here in Panama but we didn't have an address for her, which is not unusual for our clients. She used a post office box."

"Did she pay the law firm with checks?"

"No, she did wire transfers from an account at *Banco Nacional De Panama.*"

"What else can you tell us about her?"

"Not much. We kept the corporate records and the trust documents. Oh, she did come into the office a few times."

VanDerlies' eyes got wide at that.

"Did you actually see her?"

"Yes, a couple of times. Once I brought coffee to her in the conference room."

"What did she look like?"

"Oh, she was a very attractive young woman, actually quite beautiful, tall, dark haired, huge blue eyes, quite lovely. She was very pale skinned but she spoke Spanish the whole time, although her accent wasn't Panamanian, it was more Spanish, like mine."

"How old would you say she was?"

"Quite young, I would say, probably mid to late twenties."

"Do you know if there was anyone else involved with Medusa?"

"The corporate records don't show anyone else but the last time she came in, not long before she terminated her relationship with the firm, she came in with a man."

"Can you describe him? Do you know who he was?"

"He was maybe five foot nine, dark hair, clean-shaven, medium build, a little older than her, maybe mid-thirties. She described him as her '*novio.*' She laughed after she said it so I don't know if she was serious. He spoke no Spanish. I'm pretty sure he was American. She was the one to conduct all the business in Spanish. He just kind of sat there. I'm not sure he knew what was going on."

"When did this Maria Guisado terminate the firm's services?"

"Not too long after that last meeting. Maybe a couple of months."

"Do you have any idea why?"

"I can only guess, but I got the feeling it was connected to the information I gave to you people. You were asking about the Cayman Island accounts connected to the corporation and I gave the FBI all the information I had. I figured she found out somehow and wanted to remove the links. I was afraid I was going to get fired. I guess she never made the connection between the leaks and me."

"Did you ever have the impression she was a front for an organization of some sort?"

"I really couldn't tell. Except for that one time she always came in alone. There were no references to any other individual in the trust or corporate documents."

"Do you have any idea where the money came from for the corporation?"

"No, it all flowed in from the Cayman accounts. We had no access to the account information. It could have been anything. I believe she told them she was a consultant but we never knew what it was she consulted on."

"Was there a lot of money?"

"No idea. We knew about the Cayman accounts which were connected to the corporation but the money flowed into local banks, not through us. Judging by the young woman's clothes she was doing pretty well."

"One last thing. I have a picture here," he said pulling out an eight by ten black and white still taken from the hotel surveillance file. He handed it over to her and she looked at it for a few seconds.

"Well, it's pretty blurry. I never saw her wear her hair in a bun like that, it was always loose and flowing. Also, she never wore glasses. It could be her, yes I think it could be."

VanDerlies looked at Haden triumphantly.

"You have been a great help to us, Senorita Bruguera. We are most grateful to you for all your help on this matter."

"I can expect a deposit in my account of the usual amount?"

"Yes, of course."

"What is this woman supposed to have done that you are so interested in her?"

Haden was about to tell her the matter was under investigation and they could not divulge any more when VanDerlies spoke first.

"She may have been involved in a lucrative and high-profile murder for hire scheme from which your firm helped her hide the profits. The woman nodded, glanced at both of them, gathered her purse and left.

"Why did you tell her what we are on to? For all we know it could get back to the very people we are trying to find."

"I hope it does exactly that," said VanDerlies grinning.

Chapter Eleven
Sainte-Marie, Island of Guadeloupe

It was now several weeks since Amelie started working for the woman who called herself Ariella. For most of that time the woman had not been around. The house was empty and quiet. Amelie dusted and cleaned the big house every day. She noticed that the woman's closet had some very nice clothes which she imagined were expensive. The kitchen contained very little food but the refrigerator was filled with bottles of champagne. There was an expensive looking stereo with huge wooden boxes for speakers. The components had clear glass tubes which lit up when the stereo was turned on and there was a device she had never seen before, the woman called it a 'turntable' and showed her how to work it. She told Amelie that when she was gone on her travels Amelie could play music if she liked while she worked.

At lunch time when she was alone Amelie would sit out on the broad stone terrace while watching the surf roll up on the beach below. When the woman left, she gave Amelie her pay in advance.

"I'm trusting you," she said "and I expect the place to be in perfect condition when I get back."

She never told Amelie when she was coming back. She would just suddenly show up, immediately change into a bathing suit and take a bottle of champagne and an ice bucket down to the beach. She barely said hello to Amelie. At lunch time she would bring a tray with grilled fish and fresh cut fruit down to her on the beach. Usually, she would bring a fresh bottle of champagne too. Amelie was amazed at how much the woman drank but she never seemed to be affected by the alcohol at all.

Twice the woman drove her into Goyave for groceries and to restock her supply of champagne. Amelie was shocked when she saw that each bottle was over two hundred Euros. During the periods when she was at the villa the woman went through several thousand Euros worth of champagne.

While she was at the beach the woman read voraciously. Amelie noticed sometimes the books were in Spanish and sometimes in English. Twice, while the woman was away, a delivery with boxes of books came. Amelie had been told to simply have the boxes placed in the library. When the woman was in the house, she usually was in her office, which Amelie was forbidden to enter under any circumstances, or in the library unpacking boxes sorting then shelving books. At these times the house was filled with music, almost always American jazz played on thin black discs placed on the turntable. There were never any visitors and Amelie could not remember the woman ever receiving a phone call. In fact, she was not certain the woman even had a cell phone.

All in all, Amelie was happy with the job although she found the woman quite peculiar even for a *blanc*. Most white people were imperious and patronizing but this woman, when she seemed aware of Amelie's existence, was pleasant and friendly. She often asked after Amelie's mother and expressed curiosity about her love life.

"Men are useful," she would tell her, "They have their place, just never get too attached."

Which led Amelie to wonder even more about the woman's own romantic attachments. The merchants in Goyave were certainly aware of her, "*la belle Americaine*" they called her. Yet, Amelie could find no indication of a lover, of either sex, in the woman's life.

Occasionally, when the woman spent time in her office, Amelie glimpsed a large desk with a computer monitor when the door opened briefly during one of these sessions. Often, after a prolonged session in the office, the woman would announce she was leaving. She would hand Amelie her wages in cash for the next few weeks and instruct her to take good care of the house while she was gone. Within hours a taxi would appear and the woman would drive off clutching a small carry-on bag.

Chapter Twelve
Los Angeles, California

It was a Santa Ana day in L.A. The hot, dry desert wind swept through the streets of the city like a vengeful specter. In the Pico-Union District, it was ninety-two degrees, the air felt like the interior of a convection oven. Louis Saldana drove his blue Camaro down Twenty-Fourth Street looking for a parking place close to La Cocinita, a Salvadoran joint known for its fluffy, cheesy *pupusas*. It was also a gathering place for members of Barrio18 of which Louis was senior member.

"Louis *mi hermano*," Raymundo greeted him.

Louis joined a small group sitting at a metal table with bottles of *Cerveza Suprema*. There was Raymundo, with whom Louis went to school and joined Barrio18 together, Jesus, barely nineteen and jangly with nerves. Borruca a muscle guy who provided security wherever the gang elders went and Rubio, *El Ejecutor*, whose calm demeanor was almost frightening.

Louis ordered himself a *Cerveza* and bumped fists with each of the others. "How is it going on the street?" he asked.

"Shit man, it's going good, real good. We got more customers than we got powder," said Raymundo.

"That problem will soon be solved," replied Rubio. "I been talking to Felipe from the *Urbenos*. We got product coming in two days in a cargo ship dockin' in Long Beach. I need some dudes to help unload but it should be on the street by the beginning of next week."

Louis nodded.

"Any trouble from the Crips?" he asked.

"No, we being very careful, boss, and we're ready for them if they show up," said Rubio.

"On the street are we getting hassled by the Crips?" asked Louis.

"Nah," said Raymundo "I got to admit I'm a little surprised. They got to be on to what we are doing. I don't get it."

"Well, we stay off their turf and maybe it stays peaceful?" offered Louis.

"Shit, two months ago it was all their turf. Anybody wanted powder they had to go through Crips street vendors," said Raymundo. "Now they got competition."

"Nobody wants a gang war, not us, not the Crips. Too much violence could fuck this whole thing up, get too much attention, force the *policia* to do their jobs for a change," laughed Louis. They ordered a platter of Salvadoran *chorizos* and a side of *yucca frita* to go along with another order of *pupusas* stuffed with cheese and pork. There was another round of *Supremas* and the talk turned to girls and rap music. Louis leaned back in his chair. At last, he had made the Colombian connection for Barrio18 he always dreamed of. Good Colombian powder to slake the nose needs of L.A.'s elite. Louis was already thinking of the things he would buy; a hot car, a new pad in Eagle Rock, clothes, shoes, money for clubbing. Best of all if you had *dinero* you had women, a fucking harem if you wanted it.

The only problem might be the Crips. For several years they had the corner on the white powder market with product coming from the Medellin cartel. In the last year a group in Colombia from the Pacific coast, the *Urbenos,* made up mostly of guys from right wing militias began dealing in competition with Medellin. The peace treaty between the Colombian government and the left-wing FARC guerillas freed up the right-wing militias which formed to help the army fight FARC. The militias began small time dealing in cocaine to finance their fight against FARC. With the fight over, they formed *Urbenos* to continue and expand the cocaine trade. They had the weapons and manpower to protect the business in Colombia. All they needed was the distribution network in the number one cocaine consumption nation in the world, the USA, to thrive. That is where Barrio18 came in. A mix of Central Americans and Mexicans, many born in the U.S. from immigrant parents, they knew their way around the city and spoke the language. It was a perfect partnership. The only problem was the Crips and the Medellin cartel. Louis was staying armed and he kept Borruca close at hand. So far, the Crips had been quiet but he knew he had to be ready.

Chapter Thirteen
Panama City, Panama

VanDerlies was quite pleased with the interview with the Bruguera woman. "The fact that she came to a meeting with an older man supports my theory that she wasn't doing any of this alone."

"Maybe she was the brains of the operation?" commented Haden dryly.

"I rather doubt that. Maybe she spoke Spanish and her boss did not so she conducted the meeting on his behalf."

"Everyone in that law firm spoke English, even the clerks like Bruguera. He could have conducted the business as easily in English. Maybe they spoke Spanish precisely so he wouldn't know what was going on?"

"Well, at least we know there is a link between Diaz' murder and Medusa. That link is the woman she identified from our surveillance video."

"It wasn't the strongest ID I've ever seen," mused Haden.

"For our purposes it's good enough. We were already pretty certain Diaz' murder was linked with the investigation you were conducting with him. This provides confirmation. We're just not entirely sure what we're dealing with. We do know it is some kind of murder for hire operation and that there were at least two people involved. I say we celebrate tonight. It's on me, maybe champagne?"

It was late afternoon. When they got back to the hotel. They went into the lobby bar. It was dark and cool with ultra-efficient air conditioning. There was not no one else in the bar besides the bartender and a bored cocktail waitress. VanDerlies ordered a bottle of Mumm Napa.

Haden rarely drank and the champagne quickly went to her head. VanDerlies did not seem to have much more tolerance. After three glasses they were both slurring their words and laughing about the poor clerk they just interviewed. "She had no idea she was serving coffee to someone involved in brutal killings," VanDerlies giggled.

"That law firm must have its share of notorious clients but Medusa would have to be the worst," laughed Haden.

"You've really surprised me. You've been a big help, had some good ideas about the investigation. I didn't expect such an attractive woman to be such a good investigator."

Despite herself Haden was flattered. Maybe it was the champagne but any compliment from a sexist like VanDerlies was a powerful compliment. Besides, she didn't mind being called attractive even by an old twerp like VanDerlies. He continued laughing about Bruguera's appearance and the abject corruption of her employers helping tax evaders, cheaters, even murderers hide and keep their money.

When the bottle was empty, they drifted together up to their rooms. They had an early morning flight back to New York. Haden's last memory was of stumbling into the elevator. Her next moment of consciousness was seven hours later when she found herself naked in bed next to an equally naked VanDerlies. She was not even sure whose room they were in. There was barely time for them to check out and catch their flight.

Chapter Fourteen
Medellin, Colombia

There were neighborhoods of Medellin that were as primitive as encampments in the wilderness. Plywood shacks with dirt floors, no plumbing or electricity. It was in such a neighborhood that Arturo Escalante grew up. He was in school just long enough to learn to read and write before he was recruited by a local street gang. The gang did work for the original Medellin cartel. Arturo grew up revering Pablo Escobar. After Escobar was killed the major drug trade moved to the Cali cartel but there was still plenty of activity among the smaller cartels that replaced Escobar's organization. Eventually, a loose confederation of smaller operators formed a new Medellin cartel. Arturo rose through the ranks to become one of its leaders. A tall thin man with dark skin and a brushy black mustache he was known as the most ruthless of the cartel leaders and the one most fond of violence.

Today Arturo was meeting with Carlos Bonilla, a lawyer from Bogota who had become chief counselor to the cartel. Arturo disliked Bonilla, who came from an old and aristocratic family, educated in Spain and connected to the highest levels of power in the capitol. Arturo grudgingly admitted that Bonilla's advice was usually good so he learned to listen. The subject of the meeting was the competition coming from *Los Urbenos*, the Pacific Coast gang that formed from the remnants of several right-wing militias after the peace agreement between the government and FARC. In particular the concern was the competition coming in Los Angeles, California as *Los Urbenos* found a local gang to be distributors in the second biggest cocaine market in the United States.

They were to meet in a small restaurant, Los Colondrena, known for its pork dishes. It was a workingman's restaurant with black and white tile floors, wooden booths on the perimeter where a discrete conversation could be held. The smell of frying pork filled the dining room. Arturo got there first. Bonilla was always late. Aturo ordered some fried pork belly, the source of the aroma from the kitchen, and a Pilsen beer, the local Medellin brew. The food and beer had already arrived by the time Bonilla walked in, a slender gray-haired man in his mid-forties with a pencil thin gray mustache wearing a pale blue linen suit, white cotton shirt and pink tie. Arturo thought the outfit absurd but realized it had probably been paid for by the cartel as Bonilla's fees were steep and he had few other clients. As he approached the table Bonilla appeared to be sniffing the air as if he encountered an unpleasant aroma. He briefly looked around the restaurant with disapproval. "Is this the only place you could find for us to meet?" he asked.

"I like it. The beer is cold and their pork belly is perfect. Besides, it's a workingman's café. Nobody will bother us here and we don't need to worry about being overheard."

"We could have met in my club in Bogota."

"Too risky. Who knows who would be overhearing our conversation in a place like that? Maybe a cabinet minister or prosecutor? No one like that here."

"So, what do we need to discuss?"

"Have a Pilsen, it's on me. We need to talk about *Los Urbenos*. They are threatening our livelihood."

"*Los Urbenos* are a fact of life right now. They are not going away. They have many friends in the national legislature among right wing members. Remember they were the ones in the jungle fighting FARC while you and your friends were rolling in cash from selling *coca*. Maybe what we can talk about is Los Angeles where they are making inroads to your California sales."

"Yeah, we tell the Crips to hit those Barrio18 fuckers hard. Really fuck them up, you know?"

"Start a gang war in Los Angeles over our *coca*? That would attract a lot of attention. What about instead a surgical strike? Aim for the head of the snake. Make it bloody to make a point but limit the mayhem?"

"How do we do that?"

"We have a killer in the United States who has been doing work for us." Arturo pushed the plate of pork belly towards Bonilla but he just shook his head and pushed it back. "This killer is really good, good enough to hit the Barrio18 leaders without a complete massacre of its members leaving them leaderless. Crips can handle any attempt at retribution if the Barrio boys are disorganized and confused."

"Might work. Might still start a gang war."

"Well, let's start with the surgical strike and see what happens."

Chapter Fifteen
New York City

Neither Haden nor VanDerlies had much to say to each other on the way back from Panama. Just before the plane was about to land at JFK VanDerlies said, "Look, about last night, can we just forget about it. I mean I don't want this to devolve into a sexual harassment thing. We were both drunk and clueless. It was unprofessional and shouldn't have happened. We can still work together. Look, Haden, you're a good detective, I'll give you that and maybe my views on women have been a little harsh . . ."

"You think?"

"All I'm saying is let's not let what happened get in the way of conducting this investigation in the best way possible and getting this killer."

"It's okay. What happened last night was as much my fault as it was yours. I'm not filing a complaint or anything. I'm glad you still want to work together because this investigation means a lot to me both professionally and personally so let's let it rest."

"Thank god, I don't think I could survive one more complaint. They'd terminate my contract and send me packing if there was even a hint of inappropriate behavior."

"That bad, huh. You make a habit of getting women drunk and dragging them to your hotel room where they wake up naked and violated?"

"I don't want to talk about it."

The plane landed and they caught a cab to FBI headquarters on Federal Square. As soon as they checked in a clerk told VanDerlies, "Research has some info on that facial recognition you requested last week, you should go down and check it out."

They took the elevator to a subbasement level and entered a room full of cubicles with individual computer operators busily tapping at keyboards. The unit manager checked a print out for them.

"Yes, you got not just one match but two individual matches. An Amy Zyler and Ariella Blumkin. VanDerlies checked the paperwork to read that the match for Amy Zyler came from a photo on a California driver's license listing an address in west Los Angeles. The Ariella Blumkin match was from an old high school year book photo submitted in a missing person investigation in the South Bay branch of the Los Angeles FBI office.

VanDerlies grabbed a computer in an empty cubicle and went to work while Haden looked on. The photo of Amy Zyler, slightly out of focus and off center, showed a woman in her mid-twenties with long, jet black hair, large blue eyes and pale skin. The black and white yearbook photo of Ariella Blumkin appeared to be the same woman a few years younger with less make-up and a cheap haircut. Further research showed Blumkin graduated magna cum laude from UCLA. A newspaper article a few years before mentioned her as a survivor of a massacre of her family; mother, brother and grandfather. Other than that, there was no information on Ariella Blumkin. No driver's license, tax return, address, phone number, work history, ownership of cars or real property. Her social security number had been dormant for over a decade. After graduating from UCLA, Blumkin ceased to exist.

The record on Amy Zyler was more substantial. She had a social security number and filed state and federal tax returns for five consecutive years. She worked as an independent contractor for a Nayk Corporation. Even though Zyler's social security number had been assigned while Blumkin was still in college, it was impossible to escape the conclusion that Blumkin had, for some reason, become Zyler.

A deeper dive into Nayk Corporation showed that it owned substantial real estate throughout Los Angeles County. However, there was no record of any employees for the corporation. It was wholly owned by a Panamanian corporation, Arana, SA.

Haden admired how adeptly VanDerlies penetrated data bases to pull out information on the two women. He had quick hands and knew exactly where to go to get the information he wanted. There was no phone number, either land line or mobile for Amy Zyler. "I think we need to surprise her," said VanDerlies with a smile. "A trip to L.A.?"

"Well," said Haden, "at least the weather should be good."

Chapter Sixteen
Westlake Village, California

Margery and Ted Asseyad walked every night with their four children in their Westlake Village neighborhood. They liked crossing over from their development to the open space on the other side of Triunfo Canyon Road. As they walked through the crosswalk on this warm, windy night eleven-year-old Darren and nine-year-old Carl were in the lead. Six-year-old Theresa was on her scooter next to Ted and Margery pushed nine-month-old Terry in a stroller behind the others.

A white Mercedes suddenly blasted out of the night. Margery screamed, jumping with the stroller toward the curb. Ted grabbed Theresa off her scooter and scrambled out of the way as the Mercedes, never slowing, plowed into the two boys in the middle of the cross walk. Darren went flying, landing on the sidewalk with a sickening thud. Carl was caught on the bumper of the Mercedes, carried for almost one hundred yards when the Mercedes abruptly screeched to a halt, backed up, ejecting Carl, leaving him lying on the road in front of the car, which promptly accelerated driving right over Carl off into the night.

While Margery screamed Ted fumblingly dialed 911. In what seemed an eternity police and paramedic units finally arrived. Darren was transported to the hospital but Carl was declared dead. The Los Angeles County Sherriff deputies who responded got a description of the Mercedes from the shaken parents. Within an hour a matching vehicle was stopped. There was significant damage to the front end of the car. The driver, Rebecca Bergman, received a breathalyzer test that placed her well over the legal limit for blood alcohol. She was taken into custody and booked for vehicular manslaughter, driving while intoxicated, and fleeing the scene of an accident. Later the next morning Darren died.

Rebecca Bergman was the forty-seven-year-old wife of Doctor Paul Bergman founder of the Los Angeles Bergman Burn Center. She was socially prominent, known for her involvement with charities, had previously been named the Woman of The Year by a local organization. The morning after the accident she appeared in court represented by a lawyer. She pleaded not guilty and was released on two million dollars bail which was promptly posted. She walked out of court and went home.

Two months later no trial had been scheduled. No one could tell Ted and Margery the status of the criminal case against Rebecca Bergman.

Ted went to his uncle Younus, a wealthy man who owned a chain of gas station convenience stores. "Uncle," he said "we are shattered by losing our two boys, we can't sleep, we have no appetite. Margery just cries and cries every day. Our two girls don't understand what happened, why their brothers are gone and why their parents are so sad. We are ruined by this, Younus, just ruined. The worst part of all is this murderer who killed our boys, she is free. We are afraid she will never be punished. Her husband is rich, she has influential friends. She is going to get away with this."

Younus nodded. "Maybe there's a way to ensure that she gets what she deserves," he said quietly.

"How would that happen?"

"I'll tell you, Ted, the less you know, the better off you will be. I understand how you feel. I think your fears are correct. People like this Bergman woman, they are not punished. The rules for them are different. That's what you learn doing business in this country. Maybe there is a way to balance the scales. I'll see what I can do. You will know if it happens. That's all I can say."

Chapter Seventeen
Los Angeles, California

The crime scene was messy. Even in gang ridden Pico-Union it was unusual to find so many corpses. Homicide detective Jesse Rodriguez counted six in the dining room of La Cocinita. He was told there were two more in the kitchen. He stood by the restaurant's front counter with Manny Griegos from the gang unit. Four of the dead were prominent members of Barrio18 the dominant local gang. "This guy here by the counter," said Griegos, "was Louis Saldana, a primary in Barrio18."

"He was shot at close range. I would guess it was a nine-millimeter, but forensics will confirm that when they remove the slug," commented Rodriguez.

"The four dudes at the table over there," said Griegos nodding toward four dead bodies lying on the floor about twenty feet away next to a table still laden with platters of *pupusas* and bottles of *cerveza*, "are Jesus Moreno, Raymundo Dorado and Pedro Salazar, AKA Borruca and Michael Rubio. Raymundo was probably second in rank behind Louis. Borruca and Rubio were muscle. Rubio is a prime suspect in a couple of murders but nothing could ever be proven. Borruca was a kind of bodyguard for Louis and Raymundo. As far as we know Moreno was a nobody, just a kid."

"This guy?" asked Rodriguez gesturing to the body behind the counter.

"Just some dude who works here. No gang connection as far as we can tell other than working at a place they liked to hang out. Same with the guys in the kitchen."

Rodriguez walked over to the bodies by the table. "Just one entry point on each of them. It doesn't look like these guys were shot at close range. I'd say the shooter was right over there by the counter where Saldana was shot. That is some really good shooting. It looks like Rubio got his gun out but didn't have a chance to fire it. Borruca hadn't even got his out yet. Let me ask you is this kind of surgical strike a typical gang hit?"

"No, not really. These gang bangers don't get the chance to practice at the gun range. They're usually pretty crude with their hits, just kind of, you know, shooting up a place, spraying bullets or firing at close range if they can get that close."

"Yeah, this looks pretty surgical. It was accurate shooting and they even took time to scoop up their brass. The way I see it the killer comes in and stands at the counter in the front of the restaurant. For some reason Louis comes right over. The killer surprises him and shoots him in the chest at close range then opens fire on the guys at the table hitting each one with a single rapid-fire shot. The counter guy looks like he was hunkered down behind the counter when the shooting starts. The killer bends over the counter and shoots him in the head execution style. He goes into the kitchen where the two cooks are crouched behind a prep table. They get shot the same way, single bullet to the forehead. Then, if I were to guess, the killer exits through the back door of the kitchen into the alley. We have guys combing the alley for a gun just in case he dumped it out there somewhere."

"I think you got it about right," said Griegos. "It took some balls to walk into a gang hang out and take out their key members."

"Let me ask you, does this really look like a gang hit?"

"Not really. Like you pointed out, whoever did this was fast and accurate. I don't think a gang hit would take out innocent witnesses like this one did. They would be here to send a message, let people know who did it. We were thinking it might be Crips who did this but a Crip hit would be crude."

"Why Crips?"

"Lately there has been some new cocaine being sold on the street. For the last few years, the Crips have been the distributors for Medellin coke. Suddenly Barrio18 is working the street with stuff just as good as the Medellin. Crips aren't likely to want the competition."

"This doesn't look like a Crips hit?"

"No," answered Griegos "it looks professional."

"Medellin would have every reason to hit these guys and they could afford the best. Maybe they thought that a hit like this would not start a gang war but send a subtler message. Anyway, just killing these guys is likely to interfere with Barrio18 operations, isn't it?"

"Yeah, these are their key guys. They cut the head off the snake. It may take a while for Barrio18 to recover."

"So, we check flights to see if anyone came in on a Colombian passport. We know Medellin operates locally through the Crips so if they are using a professional, they likely sent one of their own in. If they did, we'll find out."

Chapter Eighteen
Los Angeles, California

As the plane slowly began losing altitude, Haden looked out the window through hazy brown sky to see acres of low-rise buildings, slithering freeways choked with traffic. In the distance she could see a patch of high-rise buildings rising alone like the city of Oz. it was November and the temperature in downtown Los Angeles, according to the pilot as he announced their imminent arrival, was ninety-four degrees.

Sitting next to her, VanDerlies was intent on his laptop. Upon landing they rented a car and booked rooms at the vast, characterless LAX Hilton on Century Boulevard. Haden was emphatic about not wanting to socialize with VanDerlies that night. He seemed indifferent to her request to dine alone. They agreed to meet the next morning and find the address for Amy Zyler. If they were extraordinarily lucky, they would have their suspect there.

Zyler's address on her driver's license was on a quiet street in West Los Angeles lined with mature live oak trees. The address was unit B of a Tudor style duplex with fake beams intersecting the plaster exterior and a severely peaked roof, a rarity in rain deprived Los Angeles. The name on the mail box for unit B was Emily Schreiber. They rang the doorbell and a thin blonde in her late twenties opened the door. It was not the girl on Amy Zyler's driver's license. "Hi I'm agent VanDerlies from the FBI and this is my associate Officer Haden." The woman looked alarmed.

"We're looking for Amy Zyler. Is she in?" asked Haden.

"I've never heard of anyone by that name," answered the woman.

"Do you know if anyone by that name has ever lived here?" asked VanDerlies.

"I have no idea who lived here before me."

"How long have you lived here?"

"Almost six years now."

"You never had a roommate?" asked Haden.

"Well, yeah the first couple of years I did but she wasn't named Amy. What is this all about anyway?"

"Just a routine investigation," said VanDerlies, "Is this your old roommate?" He showed her a blow-up of the Amy Zyler driver's license photo."

"No, I've never seen this woman. My roommate was Asian, Korean-American to be precise. This is definitely not her."

VanDerlies shook his head as they walked back to the car. "I expected something like this. The address was totally bogus. If we dig a little bit, we may find a death certificate for an Amy Zyler. Our next stop, Redondo Beach to talk to the agent investigating the Fred Cornwall disappearance."

Haden was surprised how long it took them to get from West Los Angeles to Redondo Beach. Although they took freeways for most of the drive, they seemed to average no more than twenty-five miles an hour. When they finally arrived in Redondo Beach they found the FBI branch office on the second floor of a small office building in a charming beach side, low rise business district area called Riviera Village. The main street through the village was lined with elegant restaurants and boutique clothing stores. The branch office was on a side street above a shop selling women's shoes.

They were ushered into a small, bare office with gray metal furniture and introduced to Agent Daniel Holmgren. "There's not much I can tell you," he said after being apprised of the reason for their visit. "This young girl, a waitress in a Hermosa Beach restaurant, was concerned about her friend having disappeared. I actually thought she might have a crush on this guy. So, she goes to the police and eventually it turns out that this guy really has disappeared. His clients haven't heard from him, he's not paying his bills, his car gets repossessedm his condo gets foreclosed on and no one can find the guy anywhere. So, they send it to us thinking it might be a kidnapping. I talked to the girl, a Lindsay Carpenter, who played volleyball with the guy. She was convinced some girl named Ariella Blumkin was responsible for Fred Cornwall's disappearance. That's where the photo came from, the girl's high school yearbook. Now you tell me you've got a match?"

"We do," said VanDerlies "and we think she has an alias of Amy Zyler which may explain why you couldn't find anything on her."

He pulled out the driver's license photo of Amy Zyler and pushed it over to Holmgren.

"Yeah, I would say it's the same girl, a little older, better haircut but pretty close."

"What made this Lindsay so sure that Ariella was involved in Cornwall's disappearance?" asked Haden.

"She saw, or thought she saw, this Ariella woman pick Cornwall up in front of his condo. He'd been telling her about this mysterious woman he'd been dating. They even took a trip to   Panama together."

"Panama?" asked Haden.

"Yeah, I think that was it. Do you want me to check my notes?"

"Maybe we need to talk to this Lindsay Carpenter directly," said VanDerlies.

"I'll get you her contact info."

~ * ~

Lindsay Carpenter was between shifts so they found her at the Hermosa Beach apartment she shared with two other girls. A short, curvaceous auburn-haired woman in her early twenties opened the door when they knocked. She was dressed in denim shorts and a pale blue crop top that exposed quite a bit of a flat stomach including a belly button pin. "I'm glad you guys are still on the case," she said after they introduced themselves.

"To be honest, we are more interested in this Ariella Blumkin than the disappearance of your boyfriend," said Haden.

"He wasn't my boyfriend, just a nice guy who got in over his head. I liked him but we never, you know…"

"Is this the girl you saw pick up Fred Cornwall?" asked VanDerlies showing her the driver's license photo of Amy Zyler.

"Yeah, that's her, that's Ariella Blumkin. Looks a little older and a little more turned out but it's her."

"Would it surprise you to know this is a DMV photo of a girl named Amy Zyler?"

"No, that's Ariella. I remember her from high school."

"You're sure?"

"Yeah, it's her."

"Tell us about her?" asked Haden.

"Well, she was a senior when I was a freshman in high school. She was really pretty, a top student and sort of weird so everyone kinda knew who she was."

"How was she weird?" said Haden.

"Kept to herself, no boyfriend, no girlfriends, never went to parties or socialized. We heard her parents were foreigners and that her mom was strict. Once someone heard her speaking some foreign language, Russian I think, on the phone to her mom. She was good in school, got straight A's but didn't really talk to anyone. I heard that when one girl started teasing her, she just beat that girl down in the hallway between classes. She even got suspended for that for a little bit, then she was back. A friend of my sister's went to El Camino, the local junior college, with her. That's when her family got massacred. My sister's friend said she didn't seem affected at all by it. I was walking by Fred's condo one day, a while before he disappeared and I see him come out of his place and she pulls up in a gray Toyota. I couldn't believe it was her but I recognized her right away."

"Did Fred tell you about going to Panama with her?"

"Yeah. She had a place there or something."

"Did she live here, in LA?"

"I'm not sure but I always assumed she did. I'm not sure where."

"Anything else you can tell us about Ariella and Fred?" asked Haden.

"Yeah. One day he showed up after volleyball with a bruise under his eye. A bad one. When I started asking him about it, he got embarrassed. When I said something about kinky sex was how he got it he got upset. He just left and didn't come back. Fred, he was in way over his head with that girl. She was beautiful and smart. Fred was a great guy but not the sort who would appeal to a girl like that, you know. Besides, she was mean. I think she hurt Fred and I'll bet she knows where he is. He was crazy about her. He would have done anything for her."

Chapter Nineteen
Glendora, California

Younos Gurgis was a Coptic Christian who came to America from Egypt and made a success of himself. He owned seven combination gas station convenience stores that brought in a significant income. He married a beautiful Mexican-American woman and had three fine children. He was happy and proud of his success but he knew that America was a mine-field for people like him. That an immigrant had to fight to get anywhere or be treated with respect. His sister's daughter, Margery, lost her two sons in a horrific accident involving a drunk driver. Unfortunately, that driver turned out to be Rebecca Bergman, socialite, wife of revered doctor Paul Bergman, founder of the Los Angeles Bergman Burn Center, renowned for its expert treatment of burn victims. The accident was two months prior and no trial had been scheduled for Bergman.

Younos understood that in this country people like the Bergman's were treated differently. They were privileged. They could get away with horrific acts for which someone like himself or his niece would receive severe punishment. The district attorney in charge of the case seemed reluctant to bring the matter to trial and Bergman's attorney was insisting she could not go to jail in any plea agreement.

Younos also understood that money could solve problems or, at least, make them better. If the justice system would not punish Rebecca Bergman, he would use his connections and his wealth to find someone who would. He called a friend who was an Armenian gangster in Burbank. Once he told him what he wanted to do his friend asked "How much are you willing to spend?"

"I don't know, enough to get the job done."

"Look, you can hire a couple of punks to rough her up but these guys are usually dumb fucks. If they get caught you know they give you up in exchange for a deal."

"I don't want to just rough her up if you know what I mean. So how much would it cost to, you know, find the ultimate solution to this person's crimes?"

"Ultimate solution, huh? Could you pay fifty grand?"

"I could."

"If you are willing to spend that kind of money, there is someone who is very efficient I know. This person is secure, you can't be traced to him."

"He can do what I want?"

"Oh yeah. I heard he's been working for the Colombians lately, that's how good he is."

"Okay, how do I contact him?"

"You got to go on the dark web. Download the TOR browser go to the protonmail website at https//protonirockerxow.onion and open a Protonmail account. Then send an email to Nahtepa@protonmail.com. Tell him what you want. You should get a response within twenty-four hours. If he agrees you will be asked to open an offshore account and transfer money from that account to an account he will identify for you. It is usually half up front and half when the job is done. You got it, Younos?"

"I do."

"You and I never discussed any of this right?"

"I've already forgotten," nodded Younos.

Chapter Twenty
Los Angeles, California

At dinner after they interviewed Lindsay Carpenter, VanDerlies brought his laptop to the table. He pulled up case files on the death of Ariella Blumkin's family.

"It appears she never was a suspect. She had an alibi and no perceptible motive. It does appear she inherited everything from her mother, that she eventually sold the condo they lived in and used the proceeds to help pay for attending UCLA. I'm going to guess she rented an apartment somewhere close to campus after she transferred."

"Do you think she might have had roommates?" asked Haden.

"Given the high rents in the Westwood area it seems likely."

VanDerlies accessed the university archives to get an address for Ariella Blumkin then used the Los Angeles County Recorder's website to find the owner of the property. "We're in luck, the property still has the same owner. Maybe he can tell us if she had roommates?"

A quick search and a call on VanDerlies' cell phone and they had two names from the landlord. One of them still lived in the area in Northridge.

The following day they took the 405 Freeway out to the San Fernando Valley. As they descended Sepulveda Pass, they saw a broad extent of flat urban sprawl covered with a faint brown haze. The address they sought in Northridge was a small cement block ranch style house painted lime green. As they rang the doorbell, they could hear a baby crying within. "Lori Stallworth?" asked VanDerlies of a slender woman with light brown hair and pale blue eyes.

"Yes, what's this about?" she asked apprehensively.

"I'm FBI Special Agent Eric VanDerlies and this is detective Haden," he said, showing his badge but neglecting to note that Haden was an NYPD detective well out of her jurisdiction. "We're here to ask some questions about an old roommate of yours while you were in school, Ariella Blumkin?"

"Oh no, what's she done? Look, why don't you come in. I can get you some coffee if you want."

"That would be wonderful," said Haden. "We're so sorry to barge in on you like this, thank you so much for talking to us. We're really not sure whether your ex-roommate was involved in anything or not, just routine checking. Do you ever see her?"

"I haven't seen Ariella since the day she moved out," Lori Stallworth laughed, "haven't heard from her either."

VanDerlies took out the Amy Zyler license photo and showed it to her. "Is this Ariella Blumkin?"

"Yeah, she looks a little older but yeah, that's definitely her."

"Can you tell us what she was like?" asked VanDerlies.

"Well, you know she was gorgeous, very smart, eccentric. I didn't spend a lot of time with her. I think her major was Russian literature or something like that, mine was Sociology. So, we didn't have the same classes or anything. We didn't have the same friends."

"What do you mean eccentric?"

"She kept to herself, didn't seem to have family or friends. She owned a gun and she liked to go shooting at a range, I remember that. She did have a boyfriend."

"Can you give us his name?" asked Haden.

"No, we never met him. He never came around, I'm pretty sure he was married. A lot of the time she spoke on the phone with him in Russian, so we thought he might be Russian. Oh my god, do you think she was a spy?"

"Actually," said VanDerlies, "that's not why we're asking about her. We know her parents were Russian. What made you think this mystery man was married?"

"Because they were always sneaking around. He took her to hotels and they were always meeting at odd times. She wouldn't talk about him, not at all. Seemed strange."

"So, what happened? Did she move in with him or something?"

"It was weird. All of a sudden, toward the end of her senior year they must have broken up. The phone calls and late-night meetings stopped and she slept in her own bed every night after that. So, we never knew who he was and never knew what happened."

"So, when did she move out?" asked Haden.

"Right after graduation. She said she had a job with some trading house that did a lot of business with Russia. Never saw or heard from her after that."

"Does the name Amy Zyler ring a bell for you?" queried VanDerlies. "Maria Guisado?"

"No. Never heard of either of them before."

Haden and VanDerlies finished their coffee and started gathering their things to go.

"Thank you so very much, Lori, you have been a big help," said Haden as she walked toward the door. "Oh, one last thing, I don't suppose Ariella spoke any Spanish, did she?"

"Funny, as a matter of fact she was really fluent in Spanish. She was good at languages. Friends who were native Spanish speakers said she had no accent."

Chapter Twenty-One
Saint-Marie, Guadeloupe

It rained almost every afternoon, a good solid soaking for almost an hour. When it stopped the sun came out again. Occasionally, there was even a rainbow. Ariella spent the mornings on the beach with a bottle of champagne in an ice bucket next to her chaise lounge. When the rains came, she retreated to her office checking her computer for e-mails.

A new one came in from a man in Glendora, California. His niece lost two sons in an automobile accident when a drunk driver hit them and fled the scene. The driver was caught. It turned out she was a prominent socialite and the wife of a popular doctor who founded a famous burn center. Although charges were filed against her, she had been released on bail. No trial had been set. It appeared that legal action against her was stalled.

The man wanted justice and was willing to pay for it. It seemed like an easy job, a middle-aged woman with no security. If she was socially active, she would be pretty mobile inevitably landing in a spot where she might be vulnerable. She was unlikely to think her life was in danger even though it seemed to Ariella like it should be given how horrendous her actions and their consequences had been. She responded to the e-mail by agreeing to take care of the situation. She instructed him to set up an off-shore account and wire twenty-five thousand dollars from it to her Cayman account then wire the remaining money when he was assured the situation had been resolved.

The sun was back out. The fronds of the palm trees and the leaves of the bougainvillea glistened with the new fallen rain. On the horizon over the Caribbean clouds drifted away. She grabbed a fresh towel and a new bottle of champagne to take down to her little private beach. Her villa sat among forty acres of banana trees which she contracted with a local farmer to cultivate. In exchange she received twenty-five percent of the proceeds of the crop. The faint vanilla smell of opening banana flowers perfumed the air.

Ariella did not think of herself as an instrument of moral justice. It was true that many of the people she killed were guilty of very bad things. So were many people. She saw the human race as fundamentally bad, greedy, antagonistic, selfish, lustful and fundamentally cruel. If the human race were to receive the punishment it deserved there would be no one left to clean up the mess. It was hardly up to her to mete out justice to the unjust multitudes. She herself was cruel, vain and self-indulgent. What gave her the privilege of being the hunter and not the hunted was her innate superiority. She was a predator; strong, intelligent, unsentimental, and beautiful. Her beauty was like the advantage a leopard's spots gave it, camouflage. The human race adored the beautiful among it. They were drawn to it and rarely saw danger in a lovely face or graceful body.

She saw herself as a kind of Nietzschean superman or, in her case, superwoman. Throughout nature the strong preyed on the weak. Lions, leopards, wolves, pumas, jaguars all preyed on smaller, weaker animals poorly equipped to defend themselves. In a subtler way humans did the same thing. The wealthy, the powerful profited off the poor and weak benefitting from their labors, sending them off to war as charnel sacrifices when necessary, compromising their health and well-being by polluting the earth with the reeking waste from their factories. She did not judge any of this as wrong, simply as the way of the human race. Of course, what she did went beyond even the ordinary predations of human culture. She was a murderer. She killed, usually in ambush, taking her prey by surprise. She never had even the slightest sense of guilt over the lives she had taken. In fact, she found the concept of guilt perplexing. She herself never felt it and could not imagine what it might feel like. Perhaps like romantic love the notion of guilt was simply a human invention, a fiction meant to keep the undisciplined and those with violent natures in check.

She was teaching herself French. She obtained a French passport under the name Marie Tremblay using the birth certificate from a one-year-old girl who died of leukemia a year after Ariella was born. She thought it might be helpful if, in addition to her new passport, she could actually speak the language.

Along with the champagne and beach towel she grabbed a dog-eared paperback by Louis-Ferdinand Celine, *Voyage au Bout De la Nuit*. She was well aware of Celine's reputation. As a Jew she should have been offended by his outspoken antisemitism. This was not one of his hatred filled novels. She was attracted by its dark cynicism and bleak staccato language.

She set the champagne in the ice bucket Amelie had thoughtfully refilled with ice and laid the book down on her chaise dropping the towel and sprinting for the ocean. Among her many attributes she was a strong swimmer. She plunged into the surf and took off toward a buoy two hundred and fifty yards offshore effortlessly churning through the waves out to the buoy and back at full speed before settling back in with her book and champagne.

Chapter Twenty-Two
Bogota, Colombia

Arturo Escalante never felt comfortable in surroundings like the Portillo Club. Bonilla insisted that this time they meet on his turf in his private club in downtown Bogota, not far from the central law courts. Escalante waited at the reception desk in the lobby explaining that he was the guest of a member, Carlos Bonilla and had a meeting with him. Eventually, a young woman with her long hair tied in a tight bun wearing a white jacket and black tie escorted him into the lounge. The room had heavy teak paneling and a white marble floor. Brass chandeliers hung from the ceiling. There were perhaps twenty or more glass tables surrounded by upholstered wicker chairs. No more than a third of the tables were occupied. The young woman escorted him to a table close to the corner of the room surrounded only by empty tables. "Senor Bonilla will join you shortly. May I bring you a drink?"

He sipped the *cerveza* she brought him and waited. The room was quiet. The other people sitting at the tables in the room, all men, were wearing blazers and slacks, most had on neck ties and dress shirts. Escalante wore only a pair of canvas slacks and a loose short sleeved cotton shirt with blue and red geometric shapes. He was conscious of being severely underdressed and out of place.

When Bonilla arrived, he was wearing a blue blazer, cream-colored linen pants with a white cotton shirt and red patterned tie. "Couldn't we have met in a place more casual?" asked Escalante.

"Sorry, this club is close to my office. I've had a busy day. I wouldn't have asked to meet at all except we both know we have a continuing problem to solve."

Escalante knew he meant *Los Urbenos*. Although the hit on Barrio18 in Los Angeles slowed sales in that city, *Los Urbenos* compensated by sending more cocaine to Miami and New York. They had connections among the right-wing representatives in the National Assembly which gave them a measure of protection in Colombia. No one wanted to see a repeat of the wars that took place when Pablo Escobar battled the Cali cartel but something had to be done.

"Marcos Lucero," said Bonilla, after ordering a gin and tonic, "is the one we need to get."

"We would if we could but we're not even sure where he is."

"Lucero has always been the brains of *Los Urbenos*. He is smart, ruthless and seems always to be one step ahead of us."

Lucero had been a commander of a right-wing militia faction operating on the Pacific coast. He made his name ruthlessly suppressing FARC guerillas forcing them to retreat deep into the mountains. His militia took over the cocaine processing factories FARC established and increased their production. Now he was overseeing encroachment into the Medellin United States markets.

"Did you hear what I said? We have no idea where Lucero is and if we did, I'm not sure we could get to him without a small army."

"Marcos Lucero is in Costa Rica," said Bonilla sipping his gin and tonic which had just arrived.

"How do you know that?"

"We, and by 'we' I mean us, Arturo, have sources, reliable ones. He is living in Costa Rica and directing operations from there. He probably thinks it's safer."

"He's not wrong, making a hit in Costa Rica would be hard. Just getting a hit man into the country with a gun would be hard. I assume he is well guarded?"

"He has five or six guards armed with assault rifles," answered Bonilla with a smirk, "and the place he is living is fortified with high walls and barbed wire."

"So, why are you smiling?"

"Because we are going to get him, if you agree. It will cost us, maybe as much as two hundred thousand American if the hit is successful. What do you think?"

"Seems like a lot of money. Do you actually think we can get him?" asked Escalante.

"We would use the same one who did the hit on Barrio18 in Los Angeles. He's good. So far, he hasn't failed us yet. It's expensive because Lucero is a very difficult target, but do you agree that if he is eliminated *Los Urbenos* is badly crippled?"

"Clearly without him their operation is compromised. He was always afraid of having a strong number two because he thought anyone in that position would be a threat."

"He was probably right," interjected Bonilla.

"Yes, but with no competent back-up their operations are compromised. What if we fail? Are we still out two hundred thousand and are we starting a war that will come back to Colombia?"

"The way this guy works," explained Bonilla, "you pay half up front and half when the job is done. So, yes, we risk one hundred K if he fails. Yes, there is a risk that if the hit fails *Los Urbenos* strike back. There are plenty of stories about Marcos Lucero's penchant for violence. He was ruthless against the FARC, never taking prisoners, executing unarmed men by shooting them in the head, burning farms of those he suspected of sympathizing with the rebels. Once he burned an entire village that sheltered a FARC fugitive. He will come after us if he survives, no question. Sooner or later, it is going to come to that anyway. Medellin cannot coexist in the U.S. marketplace with *Los Urbenos*. Someone is going to have to die. I would rather strike first and have it be him, wouldn't you?"

"So, there is real risk. We could lose one hundred thousand dollars if it fails and worse start a war with a ruthless former militia leader."

"Life is full of risk. What we do involves risk or it wouldn't be so profitable. You have never been a man to be afraid of risk."

"Okay," nodded Escalante, "I authorize the hit. Pay your man one hundred thousand now and tell him to do the job. He may need to hire his own private army to do it."

"Excellent," smiled Bonilla. "Now let's head to the dining room for a spot of lunch. They do an excellent grilled red snapper here and we'll get a bottle of Chilean chardonnay to celebrate."

Chapter Twenty-Three
Los Angeles

Haden tried to persuade VanDerlies to join her in visiting Disneyland or taking a tour of celebrities' homes. They were still trying to run down Ariella Blumkin's other college roommate and they were reviewing her UCLA transcripts. Blumkin was a straight A student. Of course, as a native Russian speaker she had a distinct advantage in her Russian literature major, she was able to do the reading in the original language.

"I may have found something," VanDerlies said to Haden as they were having lunch in the hotel coffee shop. "During Ariella's senior year a UCLA professor was murdered. They never found his killer."

"So what?" commented Haden.

"His name was Andrei Petrokovich, thirty-eight years old, a full professor of Russian literature."

"Do you think…?"

"Ariella Blumkin took two of his classes in her sophomore and junior years respectively."

"How did Petrokovich die?" asked Haden.

"Gunshot through his forehead. He was found in a hotel room in Santa Monica."

"Was he married?"

"Indeed he was, with a six-year-old son."

"You're thinking this might have been the boyfriend we heard about, the one who suddenly disappeared from her life in her senior year?"

"I am." VanDerlies looked up from his computer and smiled.

"Well, that keeps us in LA for a few more days, I guess. Maybe I will get to Disneyland after all."

"Except we'll be busy. First, I want to see the file on

Petrokovich's murder. We'll need to go to LAPD for that, then we need to talk to Petrokovich's widow. Not much time for Disneyland. Besides the rides make me nauseous."

VanDerlies made a few phone calls and said they had an appointment at the new Police Administration Building on First Street with a homicide detective named Jesse Rodriguez who worked on the case.

The new administration building was a ten-story glass, concrete modern behemoth with angles and wedges. They were escorted to homicide on the eighth floor and ushered into Rodriguez's cubicle. He was a short squat man with burnished brown skin and a bald head with a fringe of short dark hair. He wore khaki pants, a white shirt, stained blue tie and a Glock pistol dangling from his belt.

"Why is the FBI interested in a homicide that took place, what seven, eight years ago? Is it now a federal crime to kill professors of Russian literature?"

"We're interested in one of his students who we think may have been having an affair with him," answered VanDerlies.

"And is that also a federal crime?"

"This student, a girl, woman, named Ariella Blumkin is a suspect in a quite a few murders including that of an FBI agent. We also think she may well be your murderer in the Petrokovich case."

"You'll have to fill me in. I've never heard the name and she was never a suspect in the case. Now suddenly you peg her as the killer?"

VanDerlies took out the pictures of Ariella Blumkin/Amy Zyler including the one from the Manhattan hotel where Diaz was killed. "This woman," he said "was the last person to see Agent Chandler Diaz alive in a hotel in midtown Manhattan. Diaz was working, along with Detective Haden here, on a series of very high-profile murders including those of a hedge fund manager, his top aide and an extremely wealthy heir to a real estate fortune. We've tracked her to Los Angeles. She went to UCLA under the name Ariella Blumkin and was in several of Petrokovich's classes. Her roommate told us she thought Blumkin was having an affair with a married man and heard her speak Russian to him over the phone. Can I assume Petrokovich spoke Russian?"

"Yes, he did," said Rodriguez raising his eyebrows in interest. "He was born in the U.S. of Russian parents. He was fluent. His wife did tell us she suspected him of having an affair but had no solid evidence, just a feeling. We tried exploring that avenue but we could find no one who knew anything about any affair. We could never find a motive."

"What do you think he was doing in that hotel room?" asked Haden.

"He may very well have been meeting someone he was having an affair with but no one in the hotel could remember seeing anyone go up to his room and there were only surveillance cameras in the lobby. There were other entrances to the hotel not covered by cameras so anybody could have snuck in and killed him. The hotel had no record of him being there before. It was a hard case."

"Do you think it would be okay to talk to the wife?" asked VanDerlies.

"Yeah," nodded Rodriguez. "From what I've heard she remarried. Should be okay to talk to her."

~ * ~

Anna Malkin, the former Mrs. Anna Petrokovich, lived in Brentwood with her new husband, a partner in a prominent law firm. She did not work and was at home in her two-story stucco Spanish revival house when Haden and VanDerlies came to call. "I can't believe you're still investigating Andrei's murder," she said when they introduced themselves.

"Well, we're interested in a former student of your husband's, a girl named Ariella Blumkin. She took several classes from him when she was at UCLA," said VanDerlies.

"I've never heard the name. He had lots of students. I met very few of them. You don't think she had anything to do with his murder, do you? One of his students?"

"We honestly don't know, it's possible. We think she was involved with some other crimes. Pretty serious crimes and we are trying to find out if she was involved in some way with your former husband.

We understand you think he may have been having an affair at the time he was murdered?" asked Haden.

"It seems like a long time ago but yes, I remember the little things, him being out late unexplained, the faint smell of another woman on him, his distractedness. It wasn't the first time. He liked young women and he was a good-looking man who I am sure impressed the girls in his class. He was quite brilliant. At the time I was wondering if the marriage was on its last legs. It wasn't going to survive another infidelity and it felt very much like that's what was going on. I admit I was fed up and while I was horrified at what happened to Andrei, I have to admit I also felt a kind of relief. That's horrible I know but marriage with him was such a struggle."

"Did he have any friends or colleagues he might have confided in about this affair you thought he was having?" asked VanDerlies.

"He had very few friends and he was always very careful about keeping his relationships with students discreet. He knew he could get fired if he were caught. I doubt anyone but the girl herself knew anything about it."

"Do you have any idea where he might have met the person he was seeing?"

"None whatsoever which is exactly what I told the police eight years ago. They figured there must be a connection between his affair and his murder. They could never find one. If I had to guess, I would think it was one of his students. There was always some dewy-eyed underclassman who had a crush on him."

On the way back to the hotel Haden remarked "Not much help. I feel as though we've hit a dead end."

"You don't think our girl killed Petrokovich?" queried VanDerlies.

"Oh, I do, but if she did it tells us nothing about her and does nothing to help us track her down."

"If nothing else everything we've found out convinces me that you were right."

"That I was right?" said Haden surprised.

"Our girl, Ariella, is the killer we are looking for. You were right all along. I'm surprised that a woman would be a professional killer at all, much less such an efficient one. The Petrokovich killing tells us that even when she is emotionally involved in a killing, she is careful and precise."

"You remember her whole family was massacred, was that her too? Was it a trauma that triggered homicidal behavior?" asked Haden.

"I think our girl is a sociopath who started killing early and hasn't stopped. The only thing that is going to stop her is us catching her."

Chapter Twenty-Four
DOMINICAL, COSTA RICA

The villa was set on a hillside overlooking the Pacific Ocean. It was a stark, clean, white building with a blue tile roof surrounded by a ten-foot wall on all sides except the back where the hillside fell off in a steep drop. The fence was topped with razor wire. Marcos Lucero, *jefe* of *Los Urbenos* cartel, former militia leader now cocaine smuggler, relaxed by the pool with a *cuba libre.* Lounging on the pool deck were two guards with AR-15 assault rifles.

Lucero spent his mornings in his office handling phone calls, directing shipments, authorizing payments, chatting with his allies in the Colombian national legislature and dealing with his financial people in Panama. He had lunch at one, usually grilled fish with rice and beans then relaxed by the pool for the remainder of the day. Often in the late afternoons and evenings he brought in girls from Quepos and Jaco for his own entertainment and that of his men. He had a contingent of six guards, all heavily armed. They were his best people, veterans of the war against the leftist FARC guerillas. He probably didn't need so much protection. This was not Colombia where his rivals could muster a small army of gunmen to go after him. Costa Rica was a peaceful country where guns were not easily obtained. Although they often partied heavily at night, he insisted that two of his men stay sober at all times even when the liquor flowed freely and the girls were at their most attentive.

The empire of *Los Urbenos* was expanding. He now had cocaine distribution in Florida and New Jersey as well as Chicago. They started making inroads on Los Angeles when his allies there, a local street gang, had their top guys taken out. That disrupted things but he was hopeful the gang would reorganize and get back into circulation. A problem seemed to be a lack of talent to replace the dead leaders. If they could not recover, he would have to find another gang to take on the distribution. There would be plenty to choose from. It was important to be patient.

Life here was good. He was far safer here than in Colombia. There were fine restaurants, beautiful beaches, a splendid view from his pool deck and very few people to bother him. In these days of the internet and international telephone connections you could run your business from anywhere. It was a far cry from his days in the jungle hunting those leftist dogs in FARC. In the early days he was bankrolled by a few wealthy landowners who felt threatened by FARC. They helped him buy guns and uniforms and he was able to recruit from the unemployed and poor young men who had few opportunities elsewhere, the same pool from which the FARC recruited. It seemed ironic to Lucero that the Colombian civil war was the poor fighting the poor, ignorant of the competing ideologies on each side.

The armistice with FARC ended all that. Lucero, like his wealthy patrons had been vehemently against any deal with the traitors. Suddenly, the villains he had been fighting were walking freely in the open, even organizing a political party with the blessing of the government. In the latter years of the fight Lucero's militia had taken over some of the cocaine processing labs the FARC used to finance their revolution. Lucero used them in the same way, to pay for guns and bullets. When the armistice came the FARC got out of the cocaine business altogether. That was part of the deal. Some of the smaller cartels in Medellin and Cali tried to fill the vacuum created by the withdrawal of FARC. Lucero's group already had control of a substantial supply of cocaine. What they needed to do was develop a distribution system. They had the weapons and men to safeguard the labs and the shipments in Colombia. Now they just needed to find buyers and distributors in the United States and, to a lesser degree, Europe.

One of the cartels had somehow got the drop on his gang affiliate in Los Angeles. That was a surprise. Those boys were tough and careful, not the sort to get ambushed and annihilated. There would be bloodshed for a while but eventually an equilibrium would be achieved. The future for *Los Urbenos* looked bright. The cocaine supply was steady, the

Colombian government was adequately paid off to leave them alone. Eventually, the other cartels would come to accept that *Los Urbenos* were here to stay and could defend itself against their violence and hit back when necessary. They would just have to learn to live with Lucero and *Los Urbenos*.

Chapter Twenty-Five
Santa Monica, California

Rebecca Bergman ordered a cosmopolitan. She was sitting alone in an oversized chair by a small table at the Onyx, a rooftop bar in Santa Monica overlooking the ocean. She was fortifying herself for a board meeting of the Brentwood Children's Charity. A meeting at which one agenda item was to vote to remove her as a board member. The fallout from her little accident had been thoroughly annoying. Her lawyer was still not sure if he could avoid her going to jail. He was working hard on a plea bargain that would sentence her to probation and community service, humiliating but far better than jail. Her pitch to the Brentwood board tonight would be that it was a terrible accident, her prescription medication interacted with the couple of drinks she had to unexpectedly impair her and she truly was as much a victim as the two boys her car killed.

This was the same scenario her lawyer was working on in his negotiations with the District Attorney's office. Strictly speaking, it wasn't exactly true. She did have quite a bit to drink that night, she lost track of exactly how much. She did take Xanax but it never interacted with alcohol before and she suspected it did not that night. Her husband was concerned about a civil suit and had another lawyer negotiating with the family for a settlement. Her reputation and connections helped mitigate some of the fallout and the crisis manager they hired helped with the press. Ultimately, Rebecca felt it would all blow over eventually. Things always worked out for her and there was no reason this mess would turn out any differently.

The lights in the interior section of the Onyx were low and the sun was just going down as she viewed it though the tall windows looking out over the patio area. The Cosmo came and she took a long gulp before setting the sweating glass down on the table. The immediate rush of the alcohol felt good and she stretched her legs out feeling more relaxed. In the background the bar's sound system played some sort of jazz tune, a trumpet. She took another long drink of the Cosmo, closed her eyes and collapsed back in her chair.

"It's beautiful, isn't it?" said a woman's voice.

She opened her eyes and saw a tall blonde, blue eyed woman standing over her. "Can I buy you a drink?" the woman asked.

Without asking permission the woman sat down in the seat right next to Rebecca. "I'm sorry, were you talking to me?" asked Rebecca in a tone that she hoped was just unfriendly enough to let the woman know she was not welcome.

"Yes, the trumpet, it's Clifford Brown, one of my favorites. He has a lovely tone. Let me get you another. It's a Cosmopolitan, right?" the woman gestured to the waitress and ordered another Cosmo for Rebecca and a club soda for herself.

Rebecca looked her over. She was very pretty, young, maybe mid to late twenties with pale skin and huge blue eyes. She wore a simple blue wool dress, sleeveless with thick shoulder straps, hemmed right at the knees. Rebecca's fashion sense told her this was an expensive garment. The woman wore a single blue sapphire on a silver chain around her neck. "I'm Fiona," the girl said "and you?"

"It's Rebecca. I don't know you, do I?"

"We've never met but I know your husband, Paul, Doctor Bergman. Such a talented man, you're very lucky Rebecca."

The woman smiled but there was something uncheerful, almost empty, about the smile. It made Rebecca uncomfortable.

"Where did you meet my husband?"

"It's a long story, I hope you have time," said the woman, still smiling as the waitress arrived with the drinks and cleared Rebecca's empty glass.

"Actually, I don't, I've got a board meeting for a charity I sit on. Thank you for the drink," she said hoping it sounded like a dismissal."

"Oh yes, the children's charity. That should be unpleasant."

"What do you know about tonight's meeting?" Rebecca asked feeling slightly alarmed that this woman knew more than a casual stranger should.

"I just know it's going to be okay," the woman said leaning over to pat Rebecca on the thigh.

"Ouch," said Rebecca feeling a sharp prick on her leg.

"Oh, I am so sorry. It's my ring, I must have scratched you. I was only trying to say that there is no way the board is going to vote you off because of some stupid accident. It's not going to happen. I promise you that. Will you excuse me? I need to use the ladies room."

The woman got up and began making her way toward the exit. Rebecca realized that she had not seen the woman wearing any rings. In fact, she was wearing a pair of white cotton gloves. Rebecca wanted to yell at her that the restroom was in the other direction but she found herself unable to speak. Her heart seemed to stop beating then speed up at intense speed. She thought her chest would burst. She fell off her chair trembling. Her last memory was of a crowd of bar patrons gathering around her while she writhed on the floor. Then everything went black.

Chapter Twenty-Six
FBI Regional Headquarters, Federal Square, Manhattan

VanDerlies was sitting in the cubicle they assigned him. They had flown in from Los Angeles the night before. Haden was back at NYPD headquarters attending to some paperwork that piled up during their travels. The trip to Los Angeles convinced him the killer, as Haden argued, was a woman. Without doubt she was Ariella Blumkin who later morphed into Amy Zyler. Neither woman seemed to have any further footprint so it was possible she now had another identity. The last murder they could link her to was that of Chandler Diaz. Surely, in the almost year since that killing, she committed others.

VanDerlies was certain this woman was responsible for the death of Andrei Petrokovich. He had been her teacher and lover. When the two had some sort of falling out she killed him. He thought back to the killings of Ariella Blumkin's mother, grandfather and brother. Although there was not a scrap of evidence linking her to the killings and she had a credible alibi, he was sure she was responsible. From there, to the killing of Diaz, all the murders they knew of were committed for money. There was the Venezuelan finance official who was in FBI custody, the tycoon in Singapore, the rich Manhattan socialite, her two children who commissioned the murder and refused to pay the balance due. There was the hedge fund manager and his top assistant. There may well have been others they had yet to find out about. All of these Diaz connected to a single killer and that was this woman, girl really, who was only a few years out of college.

VanDerlies tried to understand what sort of person could commit so many murders in cold blood with such casual efficiency. Women were sentimental, emotional and rarely violent in nature. He always thought of them as less efficient, less logical and less intelligent than men. He hated working with them and even more working under their supervision. As he had been repeatedly passed over for promotion it became increasingly common for him to find himself working for a female supervisor. More than once he was transferred due to insubordination and once even suspended for thirty days when he refused to follow the orders of a female team leader. He felt deeply that women should not be allowed to be agents. Yet now he found himself tracking down a female criminal who was more ruthless and efficient than most of the male criminals he encountered. Maybe she was the exception that proved the rule.

On the other hand, he found Haden to be the best female partner he ever had. There were times during questioning witnesses when she turned sympathetic and managed to get more out of them than he could have with his more direct approach. As a woman, perhaps she had a better feel for this suspect. He was deeply embarrassed by what happened between them in Panama. Yet on some level, he was glad it happened. Haden had been a voluntary participant. It was not like he forced himself on her. He made that mistake in the past and paid for it with Agency discipline. Since that night she had been more stand-offish in their interactions. He wished somehow, he could start over, make it right and reestablish a friendlier relationship. Perhaps it was simply too late.

While he sat at his desk ruminating his cell phone rang. "Agent VanDerlies?" said the voice on the other end when he answered.

"Yes, who is this?"

"Detective Rodriguez, LAPD. I got something that might interest you."

"Hi, detective, nice to hear from you. What have you got?"

"I was assisting Santa Monica PD on a homicide in their city. It was a woman who had gotten into some trouble over a fatal drunk driving accident. A socialite, she was married to a prominent doctor."

"Okay."

"She had an apparent heart attack in a bar. Fell off her stool in convulsions. She was dead by the time the EMTs got to her."

"You said it was a homicide."

"I did because it was. The first round of tox screens on her came back negative, they just found alcohol in her system. Her husband insisted we run a more advanced set of tox screens on her. He even offered to pay for them himself."

"Yeah?"

"The second set of tox screens showed high levels of batrachotoxin. It's a rare toxin that comes from a Central American tree frog. The coroner also found a tiny injection point on her lower right thigh. You told me your suspect killed some woman in New York using the same poison."

"That's right," said VanDerlies "she put it in a pot of Darjeeling tea. That could be just a coincidence. She can't be the only one to have ever used batrachotoxin as a poison."

"Well, when we got the toxin results, we questioned the customers and staff then reviewed the surveillance tape. Most people didn't remember anything until the woman keeled over. A waitress remembers serving the victim and a young blonde woman. They were sitting together. The young woman ordered drinks for them both then left before paying for them."

VanDerlies could feel himself getting excited.

"We showed her those pictures you left with us of that female killer you're looking for, along with a bunch of others, and she identified your girl as the one sitting with the victim."

Chapter Twenty-Seven
Saint-Marie, Guadeloupe

The type of bananas grown on Ariella's forty acres were known as *pointe d'or*. They were sold, apparently, to markets in France and throughout the European Common Market. Ariella knew very little about bananas or agriculture in general but noticed that the flowers on the banana trees had a strange, other worldly, vaguely sexual look to them.

Periodically, the local farmer who cared for her acreage would meet with her to explain what he was doing and how the next harvest was faring. There was very little about bananas that interested her but she felt the need to be polite. Besides, it gave her a chance to practice her French since Antoine did not speak any English. In fact, Antoine, whose primary language was Creole, did not speak French any better than she did and occasionally she required Amelie to translate for her. She liked the idea of being lady of the manor, a gentlewoman farmer, even if she had no real interest in the farming part.

Her relationship with the Medellin cartel had been beneficial for both parties. She successfully hit their preferred targets and they paid her lots of money. Now, however, they were asking her to do something very difficult and dangerous. She was not considering turning the job down, but she wanted to put a price on it that was commensurate with the difficulty and danger. If they would not pay what the job was worth, she would not do it.

She wondered about her future. Since she killed Chandler Diaz, she knew the FBI was after her. They were sniffing around L.A. talking to people from her past. Apparently, some little waitress had a crush on Fred, her ex-boyfriend, who now lay quietly in a grave in the Panamanian rain forest. She stirred up some activity on the part of local law enforcement and they connected with the investigators chasing Diaz's killer.

Money was becoming less and less of a problem. She had carefully invested through a shell holding company and the stock market boom of the last few years had been kind to her. She owned property in Los Angeles that was appreciating in value and generating significant rents. Even her bananas were profitable. She did not need to kill for money to enjoy her current lifestyle.

She thought of herself as a predator, in the most positive way. But what does a predator do when it stops preying? Killing came naturally to her. Was she really ready to retire at twenty-seven? What would she do with herself? Write a book? She could not imagine life without the extreme adrenaline spikes that came from her hits.

She was spending more and more time on the island. Her big airy villa with its high ceilings, private beach and ocean views was the best place she ever lived. The long, hot days were filled with swimming, reading books in French, Spanish and English, studying French, swimming in the ocean and drinking champagne. Maybe if she had someone to share it with, that would be enough.

She enjoyed Fred's company before his conscience got the better of him and she had to kill him. They listened to music, watched movies, shared meals, had just the sort of sex she preferred. Fred was a masochist, turned on by submission and pain, both of which she expertly provided. Perhaps Fred came along too soon before her killing days were over. He totally freaked after watching her slit a coed's throat and was useless after that. She just was not sure if her killing days were over yet.

She ambled down to her beach carrying a bottle of *Perrier Jouet Belle Epoch* and a crystal flute. After a long swim in the ocean, she filled the flute and sat back to enjoy the afternoon sun as it glistened, the water flecking the cresting waves with gold. She would tell the Medellin folks she would do the hit for a half million American dollars. If that was too much, they could find someone else.

Chapter Twenty-Eight
Los Angeles, California

Rodriguez had Margery and Ted Asseyad in separate interrogation rooms. Since Paul Bergman insisted on the second set of tox screens for his wife, Rodriguez understood she had been murdered. The most logical, and only, suspects for this murder were these two grieving parents. The late Rebecca Bergman recklessly killed their two sons while driving drunk and was still free to order a Cosmopolitan at the Onyx bar. Free, at least until someone injected enough frog poison into her to kill a mule.

They had the statement of the waitress that Bergman had been sitting with some young blonde girl not long before she collapsed and died. That girl may or may not have been the murderer. His colleagues at the FBI seemed convinced that this girl was not only the killer but the devil incarnate, a professional psychopathic killer with a long list of victims to her name.

Rodriguez thought the girl may well have been the killer but that the Asseyads must somehow be involved. If Agent VanDerlies was to be believed, the girl he was after was a killer for hire and not a cheap one. The Asseyads were not exactly in an income bracket where they could shell out tens of thousands of dollars for a top assassin no matter how much they may have hated the victim. Ted Asseyad worked at a drafting table for an architectural firm and made a little over sixty thousand a year. Their joint bank account had less than three thousand in it and no major transfers out other than for their mortgage and bills. As angry as they might have been at Rebecca Bergman, they were not the ones who hired a paid killer to take care of her. Neither phone nor e-mail records showed any attempted contact with anyone regarding a contract to kill Rebecca Bergman.

Ted's family returned to Egypt but seemed to lack the financial resources to fund a paid killer. Margery did have an uncle who owned a chain of convenience stores. He might have the money to hire a killer but they had been unable to obtain a warrant to delve into his financial affairs. They had no probable cause and the guy had a good attorney. They were going to need more than just a family relationship to the aggrieved couple if they wanted to search further into his finances.

He went into the interrogation room with Ted Asseyad. Rodriguez felt Ted was the weak link. Margery was stubborn and defiant. She was angry about her sons and she took that anger out on the police. She saw Rebecca Bergman seeming to get away with an egregious crime and saw the establishment as part of the problem. Ted, on the other hand, just felt guilty.

"Mister Asseyad, Ted, can we go over once again the people you discussed your anger and frustration over Rebecca Bergman's treatment with?" asked Rodriguez.

"I thought we went over this before. It was my parents, we called them in Cairo, Margery's mom, her dad is dead, her uncle Younos, our neighbors Lyle and Carol, they're good friends. Look, we had nothing to do with the death of that Bergman woman and we don't know who did. Maybe it was some sort of vigilante who read about what she did in the LA Times or something"

"Your conversation with Uncle Younos, when was that?"

"It was, it might have been, a few days after she got out on bail, not long after the accident."

"What did you say to him?"

"We expressed our, you know, our grief we were really upset, Younos knew the boys. He understood how much we felt our loss."

"What did Younos say to you?"

"Well, he's a man of the world, you know and he said that people like Rebecca Bergman, they don't get treated the same way as most other people. They get treated special and not to expect that she would be really punished very much."

"Did he say there was anything that could be done about that?" It seemed to Rodriguez that Asseyad hesitated when he heard the question, he got a strange look in his eyes that was hard to interpret.

"No, no he didn't say anything like that. You know, to just accept it, that this is the way things are, like that."

"Younos was close to the boys?"

"Yeah, sort of. Sometimes he would come and play with them. But we didn't see him a lot. He's a very busy guy, runs a real successful business and hasn't a lot of time."

"Was Younos close to Margery?"

"Oh yeah, when her dad died Younos helped out, he was kind of a stand-in dad for her."

"Do you think he could have anything to do with what happened to Rebecca Bergman?"

"Younos? He's a straight arrow, a respectable businessman not a gangster, you know? I can't imagine him doing something like this."

Something about Asseyad's tone made Rodriguez wonder if he wasn't trying a little too hard to exonerate his wife's uncle. There was nothing solid in what he said that could justify a warrant to explore the uncle's financials. Assuming the uncle was somehow involved in murdering Rebecca Bergman, where would a legitimate businessman get connected with a hired killer? Rodriguez thought he might try exploring the man's associates to see if he might have made contact though one of them.

Chapter Twenty-Nine
New York City

Back home after the extended Los Angeles trip Haden found herself feeling some mild discomfort and nausea, especially in the morning. That combined with her period being over a week late prompted her to buy a pregnancy test. She felt sure she wasn't pregnant. In a two-year relationship with a fellow police academy cadet, now long since departed from her life, she never once had a brush with pregnancy despite a number of times when they failed to take precautions. She always pegged herself as one of those women who did not easily impregnate. That was fine with her as she had no interest in children. She enjoyed her career and knew that even had she wanted to get pregnant it would have interfered with her chances of promotion and even of staying on the homicide squad. No slack was cut for officers who wanted to be mommies. While Haden acknowledged that was unfair, it had not interfered with her plans in any way. A child was the last thing she wanted.

She brought the little kit back to her apartment opened it up, removed the plastic cup, managed to hold it upright while she peed in it and nervously dipped the test strip into the urine. To her horror it turned blue. She found herself unable to believe the test and decided she needed to make an appointment with her gynecologist. Despite her disbelief she found herself crying. As the tears flowed, first slowly and then in deep rivulets, she began to sob. After several minutes of hard crying, she pulled herself together and began to think.

Her first thought was that the father of this possible creature in her womb was none other than Eric VanDerlies. He was the only person with whom she had sex in the last twenty-two months. So, to top the extreme inconvenience of her theoretical pregnancy, her fellow procreator was an aging, misogynistic jerk. She vowed, that should the pregnancy be confirmed, she would not tell VanDerlies a thing. Somehow, she would hide it from him.

Two days later a visit to her gynecologist confirmed her worst fears. She was indeed pregnant. Her doctor, a practical, calm and supportive woman in her late forties counseled her on her options. An abortion could be performed at this early stage with medication and there would be minimal recovery time, perhaps a day or two if she was lucky. If she chose to carry the baby to term, she could probably work for another six months but she did not advise working during the last trimester, especially in a job like Haden's. She also counseled her on the hard work and expense involved in being a single mother. "Of course, a child is a gift as well as a burden," said her doctor. "It is just something you will have to weigh for yourself. Is the father someone who might be part of your lives?"

"No," answered Haden quickly and loudly.

The doctor's face registered a look of understanding.

On the way out of the doctor's office in the building's elevator, Haden's face streaming with tears, her cell phone rang. Reluctantly, she answered it. "Hey, Haden," said VanDerlies in a voice that seemed way too enthusiastic for the occasion, although he could not have known that, "where have you been? Look why don't you come down to FBI headquarters. I've got something to show you. Besides we need to strategize on out next step."

Haden sighed, wiped her tears and agreed to come meet him at FBI headquarters. It was her case too, what else was she going to do?

Chapter Thirty
Sainte Marie, Guadeloupe

Ariella drove Amelie into Goyave for supplies. She lugged a case of champagne back to the Land Rover and Amelie bought some fruit, onions, two loaves of the wonderful local French bread and some of the packaged *foie gras* that came from France which Ariella found quite passable. After they loaded the car, she looked at the young woman and decided to let her have the remainder of the day off. "Why don't I drive you home and you can have the rest of the day off. It's almost three and this way you won't have to take the bus." Amelie smiled and nodded.

They drove along the coast road past the turn-off to the Villa Dupleve. The drive took them through dense rain forest with occasional glimpses of the intensely blue sea. Here and there she could see a wooden *pirogue* casting nets offshore. When they finally got to Sainte Marie, she saw a tiny collection of cement block houses painted pastel blue and coral pink all of which had corrugated metal roofs festooned with satellite dishes. Amelie pointed her to a small, light blue house with a red door. Its two windows were covered by closed white wooden shutters. "Will you come in and meet my *maman*?" she asked Ariella

The front room of the house was tiny and cluttered. The floor was unpolished cement with a worn braided rug in the center. In the corner was a small propane stove and a sink. A torn couch and small wooden table were in the center of the room and an old television sat on a metal table next to the wall. It was dark inside with the only light coming through the slats in the shutters. The only other room was a small bedroom at the back of the house. Amelie led Ariella through the door and into a small bedroom filled with a metal framed double bed in which a wrinkled old woman lay dressed in a faded blue nightgown. Her hair was gray and curly and she was missing several teeth. She looked up at her daughter and smiled a gap tooth grin. "*Maman*, this is my boss,

Ariella," Amelie said in creole.

To Ariella she said in English "This is my *maman*, Gabrielle. Sadly, she is very ill and cannot get out of bed much these days."

Ariella bowed to the old woman and took her hand. "*Tres content de faire votre connaissance,*" she said hoping the old woman knew enough French to understand her greeting. "What's wrong with her?" she asked Amelie.

"She has a tumor on her kidney and it is cancerous. She is being treated with drugs now but the doctors say she should have surgery to remove the tumor. If she doesn't it may metastasize. They cannot do the surgery here on Guadeloupe, there is no surgeon qualified and there are no facilities. Ideally, she should go to Paris for the surgery. The national health system will pay for the surgery and hospitalization, not the air fare. She is too sick to travel alone plus she will need some time in a hotel after the hospital releases her before she would be well enough to travel. We simply do not have the money for that so we do the best we can and I take care of her when I am home."

Ariella looked around the small room with its concrete floor and spare furnishings and the old woman who seemed shrunken in her own skin wrinkled and shriveled. She surprised herself by telling Amelie "I'll pay for you to go to Paris with your mother."

Amelie looked at her in total shock. "You would do that?"

"When you come tomorrow, we'll go on-line and book your tickets and reserve a hotel room for you. I'll keep paying you your salary while you are there."

"Are you sure? It may be weeks."

"It will save her life to go will it not?"

"Without a doubt."

Ariella did not fancy herself as a robin hood, taking from the rich and helping the poor. She did what she did for her own comfort and satisfaction. She had grown up on the verge of poverty, supported only by her mother's meager salary. She wanted to be rich. She wanted to live well. Her first serious boyfriend, Andrei, called her a monster when they were about to break up. She slipped some non-lethal poison into the tea of a fellow student with whom Andrei had also been sleeping. She told him if he continued with the girl, she would murder her. He was outraged and frightened at the same time. His reaction, the fact that he did love his wife but simply could not keep his hands off the young students in his classes convinced her he needed punishment, especially since he was ending their relationship. So, yes, maybe she was a kind of monster. Was it monstrous that she murdered her next serious boyfriend, Fred Cornwall, when he tried to leave her? She probably was a monster, one who killed more people than she could presently recall. But she could do some good too. Her monsterhood had its limits.

Chapter Thirty-One
Playa Ventana, Costa Rica

They set up beach chairs and a foldable table on the grey sand beach. There were coolers of *Cerveza Imperial* in dark brown bottles, platters of cold cuts and cut fruit. Marcos and four of his body guards lounged on the beach fringed with jungle behind a line of coconut palm trees. They were accompanied by five young women who traveled south from Jaco to join them. The girls were paid two thousand five hundred American dollars each for the week-end. In return they partied with Marcos and his men and provided whatever sexual favors were requested. Marcos ordained that the girls were strictly communal to avoid fighting among his retainers over their favors. The last thing he needed was for his heavily armed bodyguards to begin brawling over some *puta*. Their job was to protect him, not fight over pussy. He made sure they had plenty to choose from. Their duty here in Costa Rica was paradise compared with what they went through during the Colombian civil war fighting FARC guerillas in the jungle.

He called over the long-legged Dominican girl, Maria, who was his favorite. She walked slowly back from the edge of the water, her light brown skin glistening with sun tan oil and her long black hair dripping with sea water. She wore an orange thong bikini. She smiled at him, grabbed a beer from the cooler and lowered herself onto his lap. The *estereo portatil* blasted a *cumbia* song by Gabriel Romero about fishermen going to sea. The relentless beat of the congas made him want to get up and dance but the sand was too hot and besides he had a girl in his lap.

His bodyguard, *Il Conejo*, was the designated security man for this junket. He sat forlornly at the edge of the group, his rifle wrapped in a beach towel. He was not allowed any alcohol or to fraternize with the girls. He was first response if anyone should make an attempt on Marcos' life. Of course, that would not happen because this was Costa Rica and Medellin's reach did not extend here. Any hard-core killer coming in from Colombia would be flagged at immigration and Costa Rica did not have the hardened gangsters that would be needed to take out Marcos Lucero.

The M-16A1 rifle *Conejo* kept close was a gift of the United States from the days when *Los Urbenos* were helping the Colombian army fight FARC guerillas. It had been an effective weapon in the jungle and was more than adequate now to protect their *Jefe*.

Down the beach a group of several Tico families glared at the Colombians, their loud cumbia music and screaming, giggling *putas*. No one was coming over to ask them to quiet down. They were lords of the beach.

Chapter Thirty-Two
Bogota, Colombia

They were back at Bonilla's club. Escalante needed to be in Bogota to meet with his bankers and Bonilla said it was urgent that they speak. Once again Escalante found himself in the anteroom of the club waiting for Bonilla who, as usual, was late.

Bonilla was an efficient fixer. The killings in Los Angeles helped reopen the market there. Barrio18 had not regrouped yet. There appeared to be a talent shortage now that their top two leaders were gone. No one was exactly sure who engineered the hit so Barrio18 had no one to retaliate against. So, there was no gang war and a peaceful turf meant better business. Escalante had to give Bonilla credit for that. Still, *Los Urbenos* were expanding in Florida and the east coast of the U.S...

They made inroads into the lucrative New York metropolitan area market and Medellin was having to cut prices to compete. While the Medellin cartels had their supporters in the National Assembly, *Los Urbenos* was well supported by right wing members and had solid support from various army generals because of their involvement in the war against the FARC. No large-scale action against the group's cocaine refineries was possible. Marcos Lucero, their indispensable leader, might have been a feasible assassination target, but he was no longer in Colombia. Bonilla said he was now living in Costa Rica which made him difficult, if not impossible to hit. There were gangs and armed factions everywhere in Colombia while guns were hard to get in Costa Rica and most crime was of the petty theft type. Escalante did not think Bonilla could solve that problem.

When he finally showed up Bonilla was dressed in an impeccable gray wool worsted suit, white cotton dress shirt and pink silk tie. He had a small pin rose set in his lapel. Escalante, dressed in a light blue cotton work shirt and tailored blue jeans, as always felt underdressed. Only his exquisite brown leather jacket signaled money to an onlooker.

"Sorry to be late," apologized Bonilla, "but it has been one of those days, you know?"

"No problem. I'm hungry so can we go in for lunch?"

"Of course, of course," Bonilla signaled one of the white coated waiters who were serving drinks. He led them into the dining room and seated them at a table for two by an arched window overlooking the street. Bonilla ordered a gin and tonic and Escalante a *cerveza*.

After they both reviewed the menu and ordered Bonilla looked at Escalante "I asked you to lunch to discuss what we need to do about Marcos Lucero."

"Last time we spoke you said your hit man was going to try to go after him. Has the agenda changed?"

"No, but it's gotten a bit more complicated. This hit man is an independent contractor. He's not cartel, he's not Colombian. In fact, we don't know who the hell the man is. I got his contact from a New York businessman I went to graduate school at Cornell with. The guy did a small time hit in New York City then did a couple of higher profile hits in Florida after which we gave him a shot at the Barrio18 hit which he handled beautifully. So, we want to give him a shot at Lucero."

"That would be a huge win for us," interrupted Escalante.

"Yes, the problem is this guy wants a half million to do it."

"A half million?"

"American dollars. One hundred and fifty thousand up front and the rest after the job is done."

"That is one hell of a lot of money."

"Yeah, but if he gets the hit done it would be worth it right?" asked Bonilla.

"And if he can't get it done, gets himself shot, or decides to walk on us we're out one hundred and fifty-thousand. That is a big risk."

"I don't think this guy walks. He's done jobs for us before and always came through. Besides if he walked on us, we'd go after him and we would get him. Nobody cheats Medellin and gets away with it. This guy knows that better than anyone. Yes, if he fails, there is great risk in this job, we are out the money. It is a gamble. We are gambling on just how good this guy is. Look at it this way, if he succeeds and we pay the full half million our profits go up several million dollars in the next year and maybe more in future years. Like any good gamble the payoff is a jackpot. Added bonus is it sends a message to anyone who wants to compete. We will get you wherever you are, you're never safe."

"I get the impression you want to do this?" asked Escalante.

"It's not my money and it's not my call. You and your co-leaders have given me some discretion but this is way above that. I can only recommend. It's up to you to act."

"Do we have anyone else who can do this?"

"The problem is getting them into the country with weapons. If Lucero had gone to the U.S., it would be no problem getting armed men into the country especially if they weren't Colombian. Costa Rica strictly controls guns and it's not easy to get them into the country."

"How did Lucero get his men the guns they need to guard him?"

"I have no idea. Perhaps he has connections we do not. Perhaps he bribed someone or smuggled them in," said Bonilla.

"So then, how does our hit man get the artillery he needs into the country?"

"That's his problem. I assume he would not take the job if he thought he couldn't bring the tools to get it done. So, what is it to be, Escalante? Do we leave Lucero in peace or take a shot at silencing him?"

"Bonilla, you know I am a gambler. We can afford the risk. If your man can do the job, we stand to gain a huge advantage over *Los Urbenos*. It's worth the risk."

Chapter Thirty-Three
Insight Shooting Range, Artesia California

Tony Demmings spent every Wednesday afternoon at the range firing his nine-millimeter Springfield XD-M Elite. Today he was distracted by the female shooter in the bay next to him. She was young and pretty and was hitting bulls-eyes on every shot from her AR-15. Female shooters were far from unknown at the range, but Tony found most of them to be tough and leathery looking. This one was young and sleek. She had soft, pale skin, long black hair and huge blue eyes.

When she took a break from her shooting Tony sauntered over "Hey, isn't that rifle illegal here in California?" he said trying to sound friendly.

"I got it long before the law changed so it's grandfathered," she said looking at him appraisingly. "Are you ATF or something?"

"No, no, just curious. Can't buy those now. You're pretty good with it though."

"Yeah, I am," she said turning her back on him and loading up a new magazine.

"I haven't seen you here before. I'm pretty much here every Wednesday.

"I usually shoot with my husband on weekends," she responded smiling.

She went back to her shooting. As each target popped up, she quickly squeezed a round off hardly seeming to aim. But the result was still the same, a bullet planted right at the center of the target. Tony had to admit he had not seen that kind of shooting from anyone. It was not just the accuracy but the speed at which she fired every round. Most shooters here took their time and aimed carefully. She squeezed off every round as soon as the target popped up. After exhausting two magazines for her AR-15 she picked up a Beretta PX4 Storm Compact, holding it out and away from her. With a steady hand she blasted target after target with the same quick action she used with the AR-15. Demmings found himself watching her more than firing his own weapon. He doubted he could ever learn to shoot that well no matter how much he practiced.

They both finished up and started packing their weapons away at the same time. The girl wore a pair of tight skinny jeans and a pink cord sweater. She swung her firearms bag over her shoulder and started to walk out. Tony stopped her. "Hey, how about going out for a beer? You can tell me how you learned to shoot so good."

The girl looked him up and down appraisingly. "No offense, soldier, but go fuck yourself."

She walked out the gate of the range, climbed into a gray Toyota Camry and drove away.

Chapter Thirty-Four
FBI Regional Headquarters, Federal Square, Manhattan

Assistant Director Patterson was in New York and wanted VanDerlies to update her on their progress in the Diaz murder. He knocked on the door of the office she was using and was directed in. Patterson did not look particularly happy to see him. He had to remind himself that she was the one who asked to see him so it was not as if he were making a nuisance of himself.

"Well, VanDerlies," she said looking at him with mild distaste, "what sort of progress have you made on the Diaz murder?"

"We have come to some conclusions."

"I would hope so given the amount of Agency money you've spent traipsing off to Panama and Los Angeles."

"Those trips were necessary and fruitful," answered VanDerlies hating having been placed on the defensive so quickly. "The Panama trip was to interview the informant who provided Diaz the financial background information on the killer. That interview identified the person behind the Panamanian corporation that received the proceeds from those murders. Diaz' killer is a woman going by Amy Zyler or Ariella Blumkin who is from the Los Angeles area. She graduated from UCLA as Ariella Blumkin, but the few more recent links we can find to her are for Amy Zyler."

"You are convinced they are the same woman?"

"Absolutely. Several witnesses have identified pictures of Blumkin and Zyler as the same person. We believe this woman started killing at least seven years ago with the murder of a UCLA Russian literature professor named Andrei Petrokovich with whom she was romantically involved. The other killings, the ones that Diaz was investigating, all appear to be murders for hire. Most recently she may be linked to the murder of a well-known Los Angeles socialite. That murder is still being investigated, but it bears some similarity to an earlier killing."

"Would that also have been murder for hire?"

"Yes, the murder victim had been involved with a hit and run resulting in the death of two young boys. Their family was devastated by the loss and the Los Angeles District Attorney had been slow to bring charges against her."

"So, the family might have been motivated to pay for the hit."

"Exactly, Assistant Director. LAPD is working that angle right now and they have been most cooperative."

"What else do we know about this woman? Is she working with an organization or a loner? Do we have a clue who she is?"

"We think she was born as Ariella Blumkin. Her parents were Russian immigrants. Jews fleeing persecution. Her father died in an automobile accident before she was born. Her mother was an accountant. She grew up in Lawndale, California. She went to high school there and spent two years at the local junior college before transferring to UCLA. She graduated from there summa cum laude with a bachelors' degree in Russian literature. She is fluent in at least three languages. English, Russian and Spanish. She had an autistic brother who was murdered along with her mother and grandfather in mysterious circumstances. Unfortunately, after UCLA there is no trace of her, no driver's license, no social security number, no work history, no tax returns, no employment history. That's where Amy Zyler comes in. She has a driver's license and an employment history, not a lot else."

"So, how do we bring this woman in?"

"That's where we run into problems. We have no idea where she is. She's hidden her tracks very well. She obviously has multiple identities. We discovered one, Maria Guisado, but she has stopped using it and seems to have stopped using Amy Zyler as well. We've put out alerts on the use of all three of the names we know about and distributed her picture to Immigration and local law enforcement. She has used disguises. At this point we're just hoping to catch a break."

"You've done okay, VanDerlies. You've made more progress on this than anyone else has. I see you are still working with Detective

Haden. How's that going?"

"Surprisingly well. She's a very sharp officer and her involvement with Diaz' investigations has been invaluable."

As he said this his palms began to sweat and he could feel his heartbeat accelerate. He could not be sure Haden had not changed her mind and reported their little liaison to Patterson. Lately, Haden seemed a bit stand-offish.

"I'm delighted to hear that. I don't think I have ever heard you compliment a female agent or officer before. Either you've changed or this detective Haden is a superstar."

"Probably a little bit of both, Assistant Director."

"Well, continue your work on this. I want this woman in custody as soon as possible. Use whatever resources you need to bring her in. we can't let someone who has murdered an agent go free."

VanDerlies took his leave and walked downstairs to the temporary office they provided him.

When Haden walked into the office, VanDerlies thought she looked tired. "Are you feeling, okay?" he asked.

"Yeah, just a little insomnia and trying to catch up on my own work that piled up while we were traipsing around Panama and L.A."

"Right, I forgot you have a case load other than this one. It's kind of a luxury just having to work on one case."

"Lucky you," answered Haden without a smile.

"Is everything okay? Are you upset with me for some reason?"

"Just tired. Why did you want to see me?"

"This is a case report from LAPD on the murder of a woman named Rebecca Bergman. She was poisoned with batrachotoxin."

"That was the poison used in one of the New York murders Diaz was investigating," said Haden brightening up a bit.

"Yes, and even better, a waitress in the bar where the woman was poisoned identified our girl as having sat with the victim just before she collapsed."

"She's really getting brash, isn't she?"

"It's almost as if she wanted us to know it was her," laughed VanDerlies. "In the end maybe she doesn't have much to lose. I just met with Assistant Director Patterson to give an update and she says to bring the woman in. We don't have a clue where she can be found."

"You've put out an APB on her, right?"

"Yes, the federal version that covers airports, ports, banks, credit cards and friendly foreign governments. We've put it out on all the aliases we know about. The problem is she seems to have abandoned them and is probably using new ones we know nothing about. We distributed the pictures we have, the still from Diaz' murder, the Amy Zyler driver's license photo and the Ariella Blumkin yearbook one. She's pretty striking looking. That works against her."

"Maybe, maybe not. Good looking women get a lot of doors opened for them, figuratively speaking, mostly by men. They get treated as if they are special and not with suspicion."

"Well, you should know about that."

"Knock it off, VanDerlies."

"Hey, I was just throwing you a compliment."

"One I don't need, okay? Look, I'm still spooked about what happened in Panama. I want to work this case, very badly. I want things between us to be strictly professional. What happened in Panama was not a good thing, for either of us and we need to get past it."

"I'm sorry," said VanDerlies looking crestfallen. "I'll work at trying to keep it professional. I didn't mean anything."

"I know and I appreciate the apology. Look I'm just tired and cranky right now."

"Are you getting sick?"

"Not exactly. So where do we go next on this. LAPD is working on this Bergman thing, but they don't know any more than we do. They have no forensic evidence, just the one witness. We can't link the identification to a real person. The girl is a kind of ghost."

Just then an alert beeped on VanDerlies' computer.

"Oh my god," he said looking at his screen, "we just got a hit on a credit card in the name of Amy Zyler. It's a car rental."

"Incredible, where?"

"San Jose, Costa Rica."

Haden felt a surge of nausea thrusting from the bottom of her stomach.

Chapter Thirty-Five
San Jose, Costa Rica

As her plane landed, Ariella thought that Costa Rica reminded her of Panama with its green forested mountains. She got through immigration using her French passport under the name Marie Tremblay and caught a shuttle taking her to a car rental office close to the airport. She rented a Toyota Rav4 under the name Amy Zyler using the credit card she still had under that name. From the car rental office, she drove into the exclusive suburb Escazu where she found the small private postal center she was looking for.

She presented her French passport at the counter where they handed her a brown paper wrapped parcel addressed to Marie Tremblay. When she took it to her car and unwrapped it, she found a disassembled Berretta PX4 Storm Compact pistol, one hundred rounds of nine-millimeter ammunition and two fifteen round magazines. She carefully packed the contents into her luggage and discarded the packing and wrapping.

From Escazu she headed west down Highway Twenty-seven toward the coast descending the Central Cordillera to the Pacific. It was a long drive as she drove the mountains for over an hour through broad curves, over extended bridges heading ever down. As the road finally flattened out, she passed rows of rickety fruit stands on either side then exited Route Twenty-seven at a sign directing her toward Jaco. The exit deposited her on Highway Thirty-four, the *Costanera*, a coastal highway stretching all the way south to the border with Panama. The countryside here was flat, lush and green. There was little development other than the occasional restaurant or fruit stand.

A few miles after she left Route Twenty-seven, she crossed a bridge over Rio Tarcoles. Cars were parked on either side of the long span. In the middle of the bridge a small crowd bent over the railings gawking at something below on the river. Ariella mused that it might be nice to be a tourist here and to take the time to stare at the river like these people but she was here for work. Besides, she needed to get to Jaco before Amy Zyler's movements were tracked.

The drive to Jaco was uneventful. Occasionally, she passed lush green pastures with hulking white cattle. They had pendulous narrow ears hanging down off their heads and humps on their backs. She saw the ocean on her right and a sign that said *Fiesta de Mariscos* and decided she had time to stop for lunch before the Feds could track her down and get their Costa Rican counterparts to stop her. The restaurant was open air, a patio with a roof, situated right on the beach with fishing boats pulled up on shore a few feet from the table where she settled down. She ordered a *Cerveza Imperial,* a local beer and a plate of grilled fish with rice and black beans. She sat back contentedly sipping her *cerveza*, listening to the waves lapping rhythmically on the shore. Salsa music played in the background, a pulsing four beat rhythm. In the heat a faint mist rose from the warm sea water. On the adjacent highway behind her she caught a glimpse of a police car flashing blue lights as it sped south. She hoped it was not looking for her.

The fish was excellent, a white delicate filet from something they called *Corbina,* very fresh and perfectly cooked in butter. At an adjacent table two men were staring at her. It was the sort of attention she was used to and was happy to ignore unless it went too far. She finished her fish, drank the last few sips of her beer and left cash in the local currency, *colones*, on the table before she slipped off to her car.

It took about twenty-five minutes to get to Jaco. She turned right off the main highway onto a road running by a twelve story, abandoned apartment building with peeling paint and gaping windows. The road curved into a busy business district with restaurants, bars, surf shops and souvenir stores lining the street on both sides. She found the local office of the rental car company from which she rented the car, parked and went into the office. She explained to the woman at the counter that her plans changed and she wished to turn in the car and pay any penalties for the early return. She completed the paperwork, grabbed her bag and walked several blocks down the street to the Best Western hotel. In the lobby was a counter for another rental car company. This time she used her French passport and her *Carrefour Banque* credit card. It took a few minutes for the Daihatsu Bego to be made ready for her and she double checked to be sure it had four-wheel drive. She pulled out onto the main street and slowly made her way through the city traffic back to the highway. The sidewalks were crowded with a combination of locals, surfers and tourists, many wearing bathing suits.

Once back on the highway just south of the last exit to Jaco's downtown, traffic slowed though a police checkpoint. She was alarmed until she saw the marking on the white sedan parked by the road reading "*Policia de Transito.*" These were transit police checking for the windshield stickers showing current registration and vehicle inspection. An officer, clad in white shirt and black trousers, stood in the middle of the road peering at each windshield as the cars passed slowly by. Ariella breathed a sigh of relief and continued south on the *Costanera*.

There were no towns and little development on the road. She passed a few large pastures full of white humpbacked cattle and several rice fields freshly planted. The occasional restaurant or gas station appeared but most of the landscape was thick, green forest. She traveled a little less than twenty miles when she saw a sign which read "*Esterillos Este.*"

Her original hotel reservation had been in Quepos, thirty miles further south but those plans were changed. She turned onto a dusty dirt road that ran between two rows of overhanging trees. The road veered left and she could see specks of ocean past the elegant homes on large tree filled lots lining the beach. She came to a white wooden gate flanked by two plaster lions and a sign reading "*Encantada* Ocean Cottages." She pulled the car into a parking area just beyond the gate and walked a gravel path between two rows of cottages with mansard roofs.

The hotel was small, laid out in the two rows of cottages in between which was a pool and patio and a wooden gate leading to a broad grey sand beach. The office was at the end of the row of cottages on the left of the path. Ariella found a short blonde woman at the front desk. "Hello, I'm Maria Tremblay, I have a reservation." The woman looked up and smiled as Ariella handed her a French passport and credit card.

"You're French, I wouldn't have guessed it from your accent. You sound American, like me."

"My father was in the foreign service so I spent a great deal of my childhood in the U.S.," said Ariella returning the smile.

"So, we have you for three nights. Breakfast is included, it's out on the patio just outside the office over there," she said pointing to a covered patio just beyond the pool. "Are you here on your own?"

"Yes, just a short break from a busy life. A well-deserved sort of working vacation. Sometimes it's just nice to be away from people for a bit."

"Good for you. Here's the key to cottage number four. If there is anything we can do for you, arrange a tour, make restaurant reservations, anything at all, do let us know, okay?"

"Thank you but my itinerary here is pretty well set."

Chapter Thirty-Six
FBI Regional Headquarters, Federal Square, Manhattan

VanDerlies had the FBI international liaison contact law enforcement in Costa Rica to let them know they had a killer on the loose and ask for cooperation. "What do you think our girl is doing in Costa Rica?" asked Haden.

"Maybe she's just on vacation? More likely she has a hit there. Who could it be?"

They got further word that Amy Zyler not only rented a car in San Jose but made hotel reservations in a place called Quepos on the central Pacific coast. "I'm assuming she has no idea we are on to her Amy Zyler identity."

"I find it interesting that she hasn't used it in the past in association with her criminal activity. She didn't use it for any of the crimes Diaz and I were investigating."

"Well, it seems as if she knows we are on to the Maria Guisado pseudonym so she's dropped that and she had the Amy Zyler identity ready to go."

"How convenient for us."

"I have our counsel's office looking into the extradition treaties with Costa Rica. They are a pretty friendly country so I think we should be able to make an arrest there with an excellent chance of extradition."

"You mean?" asked Haden raising her eyebrows.

"Yes, it means we're going to Costa Rica in hot pursuit. Assistant Director Patterson is not going to be very happy about our travel plans but we have no choice. I'm going to walk down to logistics to set up our flight. What do you say we stay in the same hotel in Quepos as Amy Zyler?" VanDerlies laughed at his own joke then got up and went to the elevator.

As she watched him go, Haden felt a sudden wave of nausea come over her and headed to the lady's room. She made it to a stall and immediately vomited. She thought she was supposed to be experiencing morning sickness but it was two in the afternoon. She wondered if the stress of the current moment was exacerbating her nausea or if this was simply the pregnancy asserting itself. She knew she had to make a decision about the pregnancy soon. Her career did not lend itself to single motherhood and conversely single motherhood was likely to put a crimp in her career. NYPD was not known for its tolerance toward female officers and their child-bearing tendencies.

A long pregnancy leave was likely to see her transferred out of homicide back into a less prestigious assignment. There was the question of whether or not she even wanted to have a child. She was never very nurturing, had little interest in her nieces, nephews or the children of her friends. She did not see herself being happy with the role of mother. All of these factors weighed toward getting an abortion, the sooner the better. Unfortunately, the present assignment working with the FBI made it difficult for her to take the time she needed to get it done. While she may have had mixed feelings about going to Costa Rica, she wanted to get Amy Zyler, the woman who killed her friend, Chandler Diaz. Perhaps more profoundly her Catholic upbringing left her feeling guilty about the prospect of terminating a pregnancy, however unwanted it might be. When they got back from Costa Rica, she would decide. She just hoped VanDerlies would not notice her frequent upchucking.

He came back from logistics with a smile on his face. "We leave at ten tonight. We have a car reserved for when we get there in the morning and we will be staying at the Costa Verde hotel where our friend Amy Zyler has reserved a room."

Haden nodded. "I'm invited, I take it?"

"Wouldn't think of not including you and the Agency will foot the bill. I'm told Costa Rica is sunny and warm this time of year, actually almost any time of year. So, you might want to bring a bathing suit and plenty of sun tan lotion."

"You talk as if this is going to be a vacation junket, but we are going after a very dangerous killer who has already murdered one FBI agent and a whole shit load of other people."

"Right. I will remind you that you cannot bring your firearm with you into Costa Rica and, of course, we have no law enforcement powers in that country. We will have the full cooperation of their investigative agency the *Organismo de Investigacion Judicial* or OIJ as they call it. We are to be met in Quepos by an Agent Juan Garza from the local office of the OIJ. He will cooperate with us and serve as a liaison. Of course, he has arrest powers and I've been assured that once he has been briefed about Amy Zyler's crimes, he will be happy to arrest her pending extradition. Go home and pack your jammies, Haden. We are about to conclude this case and arrest a vicious and dangerous professional killer."

Haden nodded and grabbed her purse to leave as she wondered if this arrest was going to be as uncomplicated as VanDerlies seemed to think it would be.

Chapter Thirty-Seven
Esterillos Este, Costa Rica

The cottage was charming. Ariella saw no reason not to enjoy the rest of the day. Tomorrow she would begin planning her strategy for doing the job. She changed into her bathing suit and walked out to the grey sand beach. She brought a beach towel, sun tan lotion and a copy of Sartre's *L'Age de Raison* in French. She thought this would be appropriate reading for a French woman on vacation. There were beach chairs upon which she laid her towel and book then took off for the water. It was warm and clear. She could see her toes as she stood in the shallow water. The waves were breaking about twenty-five yards off shore. She dove in and swam out a good two hundred yards before turning around and swimming back in. She spent some time reclining in the eighty-degree water letting the waves wash over her.

She spent the rest of the afternoon alternating between reading and swimming. She loved the tropics, warm water, coconut palms on long empty beaches, squawking macaws flying overhead. The air was warm and heavy but a cooling breeze blew off the water. The setting reminded her of Guadeloupe which increasingly was becoming home for her. She needed to be careful about getting too comfortable here. This was not a vacation, it was work.

Costa Rica, like Guadeloupe was close enough to the equator that each day was equally divided between sunlight and darkness throughout the year. Sunset was always around five-thirty. Ariella lingered on the beach watching the light fade and the burning colors of the descending sun glow to the west. As the sun dropped a few other clients of the hotel drifted out to the beach to watch. The blonde woman who checked her in sat down in the chair next to her. "Have a good day at the beach?" she asked.

Ariella turned and looked at her. She was in her mid to late thirties, short and slightly stocky with dyed blonde hair dark at the roots. "It was wonderful," Ariella said sincerely but trying not to sound too enthusiastic.

"It's Marie, right?"

"Yes, it is."

"I'm Jennifer. My husband and I own the hotel. I must say you have no accent at all. In fact, you even sound a bit like you have a Los Angeles drawl. Neil and I, that's my husband, are both from LA."

"I'm sure you are right. My father was assigned to the French consulate in Los Angeles and I graduated from UCLA, so I guess it's not surprising."

Ariella did not even try to fake a French accent it was easier to just come up with a cover story to explain why she did not sound like *pepe le peu.*

"What a coincidence. Neil and I came out here three years ago. We both had good jobs in LA but it was a rat race, you know? So, we came out here not knowing what we were getting ourselves into. We never ran a hotel and Costa Rican culture is different. In some ways the things we love about the country, the slow pace and the easy-going people, became drawbacks in running a business. We had to adjust, slow down, not get frustrated when the plumber or the electrician didn't show up when they said they would. Electricity can be sporadic, the tap water is not that clean, we had to install our own filters. The infrastructure here is not great. But we do love it. I can see you do too. Are you here on vacation?"

The sun was almost down now and small bats began fluttering in the breeze catching insects. *I'm a monster*, Ariella thought to herself, *why are you confiding in a monster?*

"Not exactly. I'm here for work."

"Oh really, what do you do?" Ariella was half tempted to tell her she murdered people for money but stopped herself.

"I'm a consultant," that line seemed stale to her she had used it so many times. "I help people solve problems. Problems that they can't or won't solve themselves and they pay me a lot of money for it." Jennifer looked bewildered.

"What sorts of problems?"

"All sorts," said Ariella smiling.

The bats went away and the sun was down leaving a faint orange glow of after-light on the horizon. The waves lapped rhythmically on the shore providing a calming background noise. "It's really hard to explain. I enjoy it. I make a lot of money doing it so I'm not complaining."

"So, someone in Costa Rica needs your problem solving?"

"In Dominical. I'm driving down there tomorrow."

"It's lovely down there, I'm surprised you're not staying closer to your work."

"It's nice to keep some distance. Besides your hotel is so charming."

"Thank you. Running it has actually brought Neil and me closer together. I know it's hard to believe given the stress and long hours but it has made us a sort of team, you know? Do you have any one special back home?"

"Not anymore. I had a boyfriend but he died. So right now, there is no one. In some ways that's easier for someone like me."

"I am so sorry to hear that. What do you mean someone like you?"

Ariella wanted to say *a monster* but said instead "A professional woman who travels and has little time for relationships. I envy you your partnership with your husband. I tried to have something like that with my boyfriend but it wasn't working. Then he died."

Ariella found herself tiring of this conversation and this woman. The sun was down. She needed to assemble and clean her Beretta, get a good night's sleep in preparation for tomorrow. She excused herself and went off to her cottage.

Chapter Thirty-Eight
San Jose, Costa Rica

Haden had to pee five times during the five-and-a-half-hour flight to Costa Rica. She kept climbing over VanDerlies who was clearly getting annoyed. "You need to do something about your bladder, Haden," he said meaning to be jovial but just making her more self-conscious.

She wondered if she would have been so sensitive if he had not been the father of the child she was carrying.

The descent into San Jose's airport was not smooth and she nearly had to use the emergency vomit bag in the seat pocket in front of her. It took great self-discipline to avoid further embarrassing herself in front of VanDerlies.

The embassy had a car waiting for them. The driver also had an update. "This Amy Zyler you are after turned her car in down in Jaco. There is no record of her renting another one. So, at this point we have lost track of her."

"Do we know if she canceled her hotel reservation?" asked VanDerlies.

"It hasn't been canceled yet." VanDerlies took the keys to the car.

Naturally he assumed he was driving which actually was okay with Haden who was not feeling great after the long flight.

"First, we'll head to Jaco and talk to the rental agency. Maybe she is staying there. If we can't find a trace of her, we will head to Quepos and see if she checked into the hotel."

Haden nodded and they loaded their luggage into the trunk and took off.

The traffic around the airport was horrendous. It reminded Haden of Los Angeles, maybe worse. They finally took a side road that got them to Highway Twenty-Seven which would take them West toward the Pacific coast. For a while as they drove an awkward silence prevailed.

Finally, VanDerlies asked "Haden are you okay? You seem subdued and all that peeing on the flight. Are you getting sick or something?"

"Or something?" The drive was taking them through a series of passes in green clad mountains slowly losing elevation as they went.

"You know, are you just not feeling great or is there something on your mind?"

VanDerlies had been annoyingly cheerful throughout the trip so far. It was almost as if he were affronted at her bad mood ruining his gleeful anticipation at catching this elusive female assassin.

"We've talked about this. I'm still uncomfortable with what happened in Panama and yeah, I am not feeling great, just a little run down. Traveling right now is not helping. Don't get me wrong, I'm all in on trying to get this girl I'm just not quite as optimistic as you are."

VanDerlies nodded and said nothing.

It was almost two hours before they turned onto Highway Thirty-Four. They followed it for a little over twenty miles before they turned off into Jaco. Haden was not impressed with the town. It seemed to be a collection of cheap hotels, souvenir shops, restaurants and bars along a narrow two-lane road. The sidewalks were crowded with young people, mostly tourists and surfers. VanDerlies found the rental car place. When they got out of the car the heat and humidity hit Haden in the face like a hard slap. For a second or two she leaned against the car to steady herself. VanDerlies did not seem to notice. Haden wondered if he would even notice if she were eight months pregnant.

The small office had a counter and a couple of wire mesh chairs and little else. On the counter were a few brochures for local tourist attractions and some pamphlets containing a small fold out map of Jaco and environs. The man behind the counter spoke English which was fortunate as neither Haden nor VanDerlies spoke Spanish. VanDerlies pulled out the Amy Zyler driver's license photo. "Have you seen this woman?" he asked the man behind the counter.

"Yes, she turned in her car yesterday. I remember because she had just picked it up at the airport and was turning it in early and because she was very pretty."

"Did she say why she was turning it in after having just rented it?"

asked Haden.

"She said her plans changed and that she was getting a ride to her hotel in Quepos with a friend." Haden and VanDerlies exchanged looks.

"Did she say anything else?" VanDerlies asked.

"No, she just paid, grabbed her suitcase and walked out the door."

"Could you tell which direction she went?" asked Haden.

"No, I was busy with paperwork."

"Can we see her paperwork?"

"It's against company policy unless you are law enforcement which you obviously are not, so no."

They left and as they walked back to their car VanDerlies said, "Sounds like we should just go on to Quepos and the hotel where Amy Zyler made reservations. I don't think she is here in Jaco and if she were we would never find her."

"You don't think any of this is a set-up?" responded Haden who found herself sweating profusely in the hot, humid air and feeling a little faint.

"There is no reason to think she knows we are on to her Amy Zyler persona. If she told the car rental guy she is going to Quepos I see no reason to doubt her. Are you okay? You look really pale and you're sweating like crazy."

"I'm okay. Do we have any idea who the person who is giving her a ride is or what she is doing here in the first place?"

"She might just be here on vacation. I mean even professional killers might need some down time and this is a popular place to vacation. Maybe she has a boyfriend here? I will say that if I have to guess I'd say she is here on business. She is likely to have a target somewhere."

"Maybe it would make more sense to focus on who the target is likely to be and head her off before she can make her hit?" asked Haden mopping her brow.

"It could be anyone. There are wealthy Americans and Europeans living or visiting here. Anyone could be a target."

They reached the car and climbed in with VanDerlies driving. He pulled out into the heavy Jaco traffic and made his way out to the main highway. "We'll head to Quepos. I'll call ahead to the OIJ officer who is our liaison. He can meet us at the hotel and help us review the guest register. We have our photograph. Even if she is registered under another name we'll get her, Haden, I'm sure of it."

They drove south for a little over an hour. There was little along the way, a small town called Parrita with single story cement block stores with fading paint and cracked sidewalks. After Parrita they drove past miles of tall palm trees planted in regular rows.

"African oil palms," VanDerlies explained. "The oil from the palm dates can be used for everything from lubricating electric motors to cooking and processed food."

"Fascinating," said Haden lying back in her seat with sweat dripping down her face.

"Are you sure you're, okay?"

"Just peachy, VanDerlies,m and please stop asking."

Quepos was a bigger town, like Parrita it seemed faded and run down with narrow streets and fading concrete buildings. VanDerlies navigated their way through a series of narrow streets clogged with traffic until they came to a sign pointing right reading "Manuel Antonio, Parque Nacionel."

They turned right and immediately began climbing a hill out of the town. There were nice looking restaurants and hotels on either side along with tall trees and green shrubbery. Close to the crest of the hill they saw a sign reading "Hotel Costa Verde" and turned into a drive running in front of a handsome, modern five story building. When they walked into the lobby a slender, dark-haired man with a pencil mustache wearing khaki pants and a light blue short sleeved shirt looked up at them from his chair and walked over. "Agent VanDerlies?"

"Yes, are you Agent Garza?"

"Please call me Juan. I'm at your service. Anything I can do to help the FBI with a case would be my honor." Garza's English was excellent and only barely accented.

"Call me Eric and this is Detective Haden from the NYPD."

"I'm sorry but what has the New York Police Department to do with this case?"

"It's a long story," said VanDerlies "but several of the murders we are investigating, including the murder of a federal agent, occurred in New York City. Detective Haden is with homicide and she has been working on this case from the beginning so we brought her along for her expertise."

"I see," said Garza. "This murderer you are pursuing is a woman?"

"Yes," said Haden somewhat testily, "does that seem strange to you?"

"Not at all, detective," answered Garza raising his eyebrows and looking at her for the first time. "Women can be just as capable of great evil as men, perhaps even more capable. So, no, I am not surprised. For you two to come all the way from New York to pursue her is remarkable."

"The first thing we need your help with, Juan," interjected VanDerlies, "is checking the guest register to see if she is registered here under any of her aliases. She made reservations here and indicated to the car rental office in Jaco that she was headed here."

Garza went over to the desk and flashed his badge. The clerk let him scan the register and VanDerlies showed him the Amy Zyler license photo. Neither one proved fruitful.

"Why don't you two check in and keep an eye out for her. Perhaps she has not checked in yet. Meanwhile, I will go back to my office and run this photograph you have to see if we have any reports on her. You say the name she is using is Amy Zyler?"

"Yes, but she could also be using Maria Guisado or even Ariella Blumkin. Also, she has been known to use disguises, blonde and red wigs, glasses that sort of thing."

"I understand, detective. We are on it. Here is my card. Do not hesitate to call me if you need anything. Agent VanDerlies, I have your cell phone number. I'll be in touch if we find anything out."

Garza nodded and walked out of the lobby. VanDerlies collected their room keys and handed hers to Haden.

"Why don't you try and get some rest, Haden. You look pretty beat." She was and she knew it. She wondered if perhaps this trip had been a mistake for her.

Chapter Thirty-Nine
Esterillos Este, Costa Rica

Ariella took the Beretta and stuck it into the oversized purse she was carrying before she left her cottage for breakfast. It was served on a covered terrace by the pool. The woman, Jennifer, brought her a small bowl of fresh fruit and a cup of coffee. "How did you sleep?" she asked.

"Quite well, thank you. I'm a good sleeper. I sleep well everywhere. The cottage is very nice."

"So glad you liked it. So, what is the plan for today?" Jennifer asked in a tone far too cheerful for Ariella's present mood.

"I'm driving to Dominical today. Just to kind of look around."

"Does this have anything to do with that 'consulting' you said you were here for?"

"It does," Ariella did not elaborate further and Jennifer took off to look after her other guests coming in for breakfast. The ham and cheese omelet served with toast and pineapple jam was adequate. She finished eating and went to her car. She was wearing jeans and a light blue polo shirt with sturdy sneakers in case she had to do some walking.

The road to Dominical was clear. She had to slow down a bit through the little town of Parrita which was crowded with shoppers. There was, however, not a tourist to be seen. After Parrita she crossed a bridge over a muddy river and began driving through miles of African oil palm groves interrupted only by an oil palm refinery pumping white steam out its stacks. As she passed the turnout to Quepos, she wondered if the FBI sent agents and if they were currently looking for her there. She had left a clear trail like Hansel and Gretel in the forest. Even FBI agents could have followed it. She wondered if they found her trail if they were smart enough to question it. In her relatively short life, Ariella learned that appearances rarely were to be trusted. The green-clad mountains, which had been off on the horizon to her east, came close to the road. The town of Dominical itself was a narrow strip of beach and adjacent coast populated by bars, restaurants, pizza joints, souvenir shops and, immediately adjacent to the beach beneath a long gallery of tall palm trees, a row of open-air souvenir stands. She had no interest in this part of Dominical. On the opposite side of the road from the ocean, high in the looming green-clad hills were large and opulent villas. This was where Marcos Lucero was living. She had rough information on the general location of the villa, no pictures or floor plans. The Medellin people told her that Lucero had between four and twelve *sicarios* guarding him, that they were well armed. Obviously, this sort of firepower presented a problem. The immediate issue for her now was how to gain access to the villa in order to confront that firepower.

She swung her Daihatsu Bego off the main highway to her left and began ascending into the hills. The road was narrow and curved often into switchbacks up the side of the steep hills. Her GPS told her to take the next left and she turned onto a dusty dirt road. If she looked out her window, she had a spectacular view of the Pacific Ocean. About a half mile ahead she saw a blue tile roof rising among the trees. As she got closer, she saw that it was a large, white, three-story villa surrounded by a white stucco wall topped with razor wire. As she drove past, she saw a large metal gate in the wall with a small speaker box mounted next to it.

She drove about a half mile past the villa and pulled over. She got out, took her Beretta out of her purse, stuck it in her belt, headed down the hillside a few feet then turned back toward the villa. It was perched on the side of the hill. As she got closer, she could see that the wall extended back around a patio area behind the house. As she approached the wall, she heard splashing and laughing. Loud *cumbia* music blasted from speakers on the patio. There was clearly a pool back there. Some of the voices were female. She guessed that during the day much time was spent out by the pool.

She followed the wall around the patio struggling to keep her footing on the steep hillside. The wall was at least ten feet high and the razor wire extended along its entire length. She could find no gaps or weak points in the wall. The villa was a fortress. As far as she could tell the only way in was through the front door which was going to be a problem. The female voices let her consider a germ of an idea she had when she first accepted the hit.

She hiked back to the car and turned it around to return to the highway. As she passed the villa gate a beat-up Hyundai full of young women sat by the speaker box. The driver was talking into the box. Within a few seconds the gate slid open and the Hyundai pulled into the villa compound. Ariella smiled, she knew how to get into the villa and she wisely came prepared for the contingency she was about to use.

Chapter Forty
Quepos, Costa Rica

Haden begged out of meeting VanDerlies for dinner. Apparently, Juan Garza came back to the hotel and had dinner with him. She went to bed early and woke up the next morning feeling better. Her room had a balcony with a stunning view of the Pacific Ocean as the hotel sat high on a hill. As she dressed, she was surprised to see a Capuchin monkey slide down the arch support over her balcony and scurry over the table that sat there. The monkey looked up, glanced at her and climbed down to the next level.

She met VanDerlies for breakfast in the lobby restaurant but only ordered coffee and fresh fruit. VanDerlies was having eggs, bacon and a huge pile of rice and black beans as well as a serving of what looked like fried bananas. "Garza thinks it might be worthwhile to canvass some of the other hotels in the area. She might well be staying here somewhere but maybe meeting her friend in Jaco changed her plans on what hotel to use."

"Sounds like a grind, but probably not a bad idea," said Haden as she sipped her coffee.

"That's why I thought maybe just Garza and I would go out to do it today and you can relax and stick around the hotel. You don't seem like you're feeling great. Anyway, who knows, she might still show up here."

"Thank you, VanDerlies. I didn't come here for a vacation but maybe a day of relaxing will have me feel better. I really don't expect her to show up now, she was well ahead of us and she would be here by now and we know she isn't."

"Well, in case she does, keep an eye out. Garza is coming by in about a half hour. You can spend the day relaxing by the pool if you want."

VanDerlies finished his huge breakfast and disappeared into the lobby. She returned to her room and sat on the balcony for a while reading a Michael Connolly novel. When she got tired of that, after a couple of hours she drifted down to the pool and into the pool bar where she sat down and ordered a club soda. Although she was probably going to terminate the pregnancy when she got home, she was not going to do anything to hurt the fetus she was carrying. Besides, she was still technically on duty.

"Hey, can I buy you a drink?" said a pleasant musical voice.

She turned to her right and felt her stomach go into her throat. The woman sitting next to her at the bar had an all too familiar face. As Haden looked at her in horror, the woman smiled back at her broadly, genuinely amused.

Seen up close she was far more beautiful than her photos. She had the most perfect skin, pale and smooth, Haden had ever seen. She wore minimal make-up, just a touch of rouge, pale pink lipstick and a hint of eye liner. Her long, jet black hair was thick and silky. She wore a white cotton sun dress with red and blue geometric designs that did not quite reach her knees showcasing a pair of lovely, shapely and muscular legs. She wore a pair of open toed leather sandals that would have cost two weeks of Haden's salary. The most striking feature though were her huge, pale blue eyes that seemed to peer at Haden with part mockery part curiosity. Perhaps most striking, however, was a sense of pure danger that seemed to emanate from the woman, like having a leopard or a panther sitting on a barstool right next to you.

"*Dos gaseous club, por favor,*" said the woman to the bartender. She looked directly at Haden. "Enjoying your stay?"

"Sort of, and you?"

"Oh, I'm here on business. No time for fun right now."

"What kind of business would that be?"

"Oh, I think you know, detective."

Haden's heartbeat raced, the woman knew who she was and why she was here. Last time she sat next to a woman in a bar that woman dropped dead. "Of course, there is not a lot you and your nerdy partner can do about it. You have no jurisdiction here and your OIJ friend is out on a wild goose chase you sent him on." The woman smiled as she said this, a broad, cruel, mirthless smile.

"So, are you going to jab me with some kind of toxin like you did Rebecca Bergman?"

"You think I did that? Is there any crime you people think I'm not responsible for?"

"We know you killed Chandler Diaz." Haden was trying hard to control her breathing.

"Never heard of the man. I'll tell you what, you let me take you back to your room for a little play time and I'll tell you everything. How does that sound?"

"You don't really mean that."

"Probably not but I wouldn't mind playing with you at all. You're a lovely woman and I'll bet you're a really good detective to have been assigned to homicide. No easy task for a woman to get ahead in a male dominated organization like NYPD. By the way, when are you due?"

"What?" gasped Haden.

"Your baby. Or have you decided not to have it? Women can see things like that, even when it's early. Who's the daddy?" Haden averted her eyes and looked down at the counter as the barman served them their club sodas. "Oh no, it's not that nerdy FBI agent, is it? Darling you can do better than that, much better, I would say."

Haden's cheeks turned pink and the woman laughed a low musical laugh that would have been quite attractive coming from anyone else.

"There is a lot I could teach you. Too bad you won't give me the chance. Goodbye, detective. I'm sure I'll see you later."

The woman got off her bar stool and strolled off into the pool area, quickly disappearing into the crowd before Haden could locate her. She grabbed her cell phone and dialed VanDerlies.

"I saw her," she said breathlessly into the phone.

"Saw who?" asked VanDerlies.

"The woman, the one we're looking for. She sat down right next to me in the pool bar."

"We'll be right there."

Fifteen minutes later VanDerlies and Garza walked into the pool bar to find a shaken Haden.

"Where is she?" asked VanDerlies.

"I have no idea, she melted into the crowd."

Garza excused himself and went to the front desk to inquire after the woman.

"You didn't grab her, arrest her?"

"We can't arrest anyone here."

"Well, you could have tackled her, or at least run after her. You just let her go?"

"VanDerlies, I was terrified, I was sure she was going to kill me, just like Rebecca Bergman," she hesitated for an instant, "besides I'm pregnant."

VanDerlies looked stunned, his jaw dropped and he looked at her like she was a space alien.

"Well, that explains a lot," he finally said. He hesitated for a moment, looked at her quizzically and asked, "Who's the father. It's not . . .?"

"Yes, you are the only candidate," Haden hissed. "As soon as I get back to New York I'm terminating it. You don't need to worry. I'll take care of it."

"You can't do that. That fetus is a human being just as entitled to life as you are. What you are planning to do is immoral. You have to let it live. You have to give birth. As its father I can't let you kill it. I have rights as a parent. You have no right, no right at all."

"Fuck you, VanDerlies," Haden said as she walked out of the bar and returned to her room.

Chapter Forty-One
Dominical, Costa Rica

Ariella planned for the possibility she would need to make an entrance through the front door of Lucero's villa. The female laughter from the pool area confirmed what she had guessed. Lucero and his bodyguards had female entertainment. In Costa Rica prostitution was legal although brothels and pimps were not. The girls visiting Lucero's probably came from Jaco where they often gathered in certain hotels and bars seeking clients.

Ariella brought a tight, short, leather mini-skirt, patent leather stiletto heels and a sheer sleeveless top. She also brought a quick release holster to strap around her inner thigh for the Beretta and a fifteen-shot clip. She could make as good a *puta* as anyone.

She had no idea how many *sicarios* Lucero had as bodyguards. Her Medellin clients estimated four to ten. No doubt they were well armed with assault rifles and automatic pistols. As *Urbenos* they were likely to be battle hardened veterans from the jungle warfare against the FARC. If they were, they would have their weapons near at hand even when they were partying. The odds were stacked against her, a single woman armed only with a pistol and fifteen rounds against a small platoon of battle-hardened soldiers armed with assault rifles and unlimited ammunition. It was why she was charging a half million dollars for the job and why the Medellin people agreed to pay it.

She paid her bill at the front desk of the little hotel and checked out. The woman, Jennifer, who checked her in was at the front desk and raised her eyebrows at the way Ariella was dressed. "Party time," she said simply, grabbed her bag and climbed into her rental car.

The drive to Dominical was slow this morning as Ariella found herself behind several slow-moving trucks on the two-lane highway. This time she knew exactly where she was going when she turned onto the dirt road. She pulled up to the metal gates and pressed the button on the squawk box mounted on the cement post supporting the gate. "*Hola quien es?*" said a male voice thought the speaker.

"My name is Mirabella," she said in Spanish. "I was told to come and party with you."

"Told by who?"

"My friend Inez in Jaco. Don't you want another girl to party with?"

"Inez, I never heard of any Inez."

"She's been there before, maybe you didn't ask her name, or maybe she gave another name. Hey, I'm a pretty girl who wants to party and I'm not expensive."

"Okay, come to the front door and we'll take a look at you. No weapons, no funny business. You understand?"

"Of course."

The gate slid open with a shudder. She suspected there was a camera in the squawk box and it reassured them to see a woman by herself in the car. She pulled into the drive and found a place to park then walked to the heavy blonde wood front door. The man who opened it was stocky with a dark complexion, coarse black hair and a bushy mustache. He wore a white, short sleeved cotton shirt and jeans. He had a nine-millimeter pistol stuck in his belt and an AR-15 slung on his shoulder.

"I'm sorry, sweetie, but we got to search you for weapons. Let me see your purse." She handed it over and he rifled through it for a few minutes finding nothing but cosmetics and tissue. "Now I got to frisk you, baby."

"I don't mind having a strong man put his hands on me," she said flirtatiously. The frisking was perfunctory and the Beretta strapped to her inner thigh went undiscovered.

"Where you from, baby? I don't recognize your accent. You're no Tico, and you are no Colombian or Dominican like most of the girls. You look European."

"Ibiza. I spent the last few years working the clubs on the island but I heard Costa Rica was better, lots of rich Americans."

"How's that working out for you?"

"Not bad, not as good as I thought it would be but it's okay."

He stepped aside and let her in. Beyond the foyer was a large living room. Three men and four women were standing around drinking beer. All of the men were armed. Other than the guy at the door none looked entirely sober. She did not see Lucero. The girls eyed her with suspicion and envy. She was far prettier than any of them and they knew it.

The guy at the door said "Everybody, this is Mirabella, give her a beer."

Someone shoved a beer in her hand. She spent a few minutes talking to one of the men and a woman and pretending to sip from her beer then asked where the bathroom was.

"I just need to freshen up after the drive from Jaco," she said.

Someone pointed her down a hallway and motioned to go right. Before she left, she tried to remember the position of each of the men in the room. In the locked restroom she unhooked the Beretta from her inner thigh and inserted the magazine. She extracted a pair of nylon gloves from the inner lining of her purse and put them on then took off her stiletto heels and stuffed them in the purse going barefoot. She left the purse in the bathroom.

She exited the bathroom down the inner hallway, Beretta in hand. As soon as she got to the door of the front room she began firing. Her first target was the guy who let her in. he was the least drunk and had his AR-15 close at hand. Her first shot caught him in the forehead. She quickly turned to the two other *sicarios* who were slow to react managing to down them both with two shots. The girls in the room started to run and she was able to get all four with only five shots. She immediately walked over to the closest dead *sicario* and grabbed his AR-15 and two clips. As she did, she heard a noise in the hall leading to the pool patio and dove for the floor. A tall gunman with curly black hair rushed into the room with his AR-15 in firing position. She caught him in the chest from her prone position before he saw her.

That was four bodyguards down but she had no idea how many might be left. As she headed toward the pool she stooped down and grabbed two more AR-15 clips from a curly haired *sicario* lying dead on the floor.

The hallway took her into a large dining room with French doors leading out to the pool patio. The AR-15 was a military model undoubtedly provided courtesy of Uncle Sam when the *Urbenos* were fighting the FARC, so it had a fully automatic function. Ariella switched to automatic and fired a burst through the French doors. Fire was immediately returned. She heard female voices screaming from the patio. Through the broken glass of the French doors, she could see a gunman taking cover behind a barbecue, a man crouching behind a lounge chair, who appeared to be armed only with a pistol, and another gunman armed with an AR-15 behind an overturned chaise lounge. The man with the pistol was probably Lucero.

Ariella pushed a heavy bar cart through the broken French door. It immediately drew fire and helped her fix on the location of each armed man. She disregarded the crying screaming girls who were huddling in the corner of the patio behind a planter. Ariella was not much of a cook and knew little about barbecues. She did know that Costa Rica had no natural gas and the stainless-steel barbecue would be fueled by propane. It seemed likely the propane tank was in the small compartment at the bottom of the unit. From the broken doorway she fired a burst of automatic fire at the lower compartment of the barbecue and was gratified to see it explode in a burst of orange flame. The bloodied body of the *sicario* hiding behind it was flung like a rag doll up against the concrete wall surrounding the patio. Just as the explosion occurred Lucero flung himself from behind the lounge chair toward his other bodyguard trying to flee to better cover. Before he could get there Ariella hit him with a shot that grazed his skull and knocked him out. That left one man with a gun. She reflected on the fact that the very fortifications of the villa had trapped Lucero and his men with no rear exit.

The remaining gunman was firing bursts of automatic fire at the French doors where Ariella had taken cover. She waited patiently until he stood up to fire another burst and took him out with single shot.

She inspected the body of the gunman behind the barbecue. He was a mess of bloody wounds from the shrapnel thrown from the exploding barbecue and very dead. Lucero was still alive. The bullet had grazed his skull and he was barely conscious. "Greetings from your friends in Medellin," she said as she aimed a bullet at his forehead.

As she stood over him, she heard the sound of high heels on the patio tile. There were four young women in thong bathing suits and stiletto heels rushing for the doors to the house. She fired a quick burst of automatic fire and they fell in a tangle of torn bodies. There were to be no witnesses, innocent or not. Bad luck for these *putas*.

The last gunman had been hit in the shoulder. There was a gaping hole where her round hit him. He would bleed out in less than an hour but she did not want to leave anything to chance so she put a round in his forehead as she had done with Lucero.

Now she had to search the entire villa to see who else might be present. Her first stop was the kitchen where she found three workers hiding in the pantry. She finished off a clip on them and reloaded. There was no one else downstairs so she climbed the large marble staircase and began combing the bedrooms. In the largest one, probably Lucero's, she found a maid. She was an older woman in her late fifties weeping uncontrollably in fear. Ariella put an AR-15 round between her eyes. She finally found one more maid cowering in the linen closet who screamed when she saw her. A single shot to the head sufficed to silence her. The rest of the house and grounds proved empty. She retrieved her purse from the downstairs bathroom, wiped her beer bottle clean of prints and left the house taking an empty wine bottle she retrieved from the kitchen, an AR-15 and four clips with her. She would need them for her escape. As she drove out the gates, she placed a round in the camera by the buzzer just in case it had a memory. She drove toward Quepos where she would turn in her rental car then take a taxi to the Quepos Marina where a boat was waiting for her.

Chapter Forty-Two
Quepos, Costa Rica

Haden and VanDerlies were at a table by the hotel pool having coffee. They had only exchanged a few perfunctory words between them. Haden was unsure whether or not she should apologize to him but she could tell he was still angry with her and decided to leave well enough alone.

So far, the Costa Rica trip had been a failure. Other than her brief, unnerving encounter with the strange woman at the pool bar they had no idea where she was or what she was doing. OIJ agreed they would arrest her pending extradition to the U.S. but their canvass of the Quepos hotels revealed nothing and they had no idea who her target was. Haden felt they might as well go home and try another angle. VanDerlies seemed more optimistic. She was sure he was still furious with her for letting the woman go. She could not tell if it was that or his anger at her plan to terminate her pregnancy that was the cause of his current frostiness.

While she nursed her coffee VanDerlies' cell phone buzzed. He answered, listened for a moment and looked at her, eyes wide. "Amy Zyler has just reserved a boat down at the marina here in Quepos. OIJ just got a notification of her credit card being run. Garza is getting a team together to go arrest her down there. Let's go."

"Amy or whatever her name is knows we're here," Haden said breathlessly as they quickly trotted to their car in the hotel parking area. "Why would she use a credit card and an identity she knows would alert us?"

"I don't know, Haden, you tell me."

"Maybe it's a set-up? A trap? It just seems too easy and convenient for her to give us a free pass to her whereabouts."

"If it is a set-up, we'll have her outgunned. Garza will have uniformed officers ready to help us detain her. Besides, Haden, maybe this female is not as smart as you give her credit for. Maybe she just made a dumb mistake in the heat of the moment. Maybe she was acting irrationally?"

Haden thought her head was going to explode. They reached the car and VanDerlies jumped into the driver's seat. He would not let Haden drive. The Quepos marina was just a little over two miles away down the hill on which their hotel was located.

They got there just after Garza in an unmarked car and three uniformed officers in a white Toyota with roof mounted lights marked *Fuerza Publica*. Garza had a pistol as did each of the other officers. "She just left the dock," shouted Garza as they began running toward the boat docks. The Marina was a cluster of buildings on the shore with a long semi-circle of docks surrounding it protected by a rock breakwater. A central line of docks extended out into the middle of the semicircle. There was a single water entrance to the open ocean in the semi-circle of docks and the outer breakwater. A small white cabin cruiser had just pulled out of the line of central docks and was headed for that entrance.

Garza and the officers began running toward the central docks. When they were fifty yards from where the boat pulled out, they began firing. A return burst of automatic rifle fire flared from the boat. One of the uniformed officers went down with a gaping hole in his shoulder. A single shot from the boat hit VanDerlies who was trailing behind the officers. Haden gasped as she saw the top of his head disappear in a spurt of blood and brain matter. His body lurched forward. The rifle fire went back to automatic and another officer went down. Haden grabbed the pistol from him and joined Garza and the remaining officer unleashing a volley of bullets toward the boat. As they fired another group of uniformed officers ran up the dock to join them. The boat was riddled with bullets. Haden saw a splash by the boat and the return fire ceased. "We got her," yelled Garza.

They waited several minutes before they decided it was safe to send a boat out to check the bullet riddled cruiser. Haden jumped on board just as it was leaving. No one said anything to her or tried to send her back. When they arrived at the boat, they saw a huge pool of blood in the rear deck and blood floating on the water next to the boat. There were no weapons anywhere and no body, just an empty wine bottle floating beside the boat.

"We'll drag the bottom," said Garza. "Unless the current pulled her away, I bet we find a body and her weapon. No one could lose that much blood and survive in the water for long."

Haden was stunned as she returned to VanDerlies' body. An ambulance came for the injured *Fuerza Publica* officer. The other one was dead by the time it got there. "You better call your embassy," Garza told Haden. "They'll take care of the body and send it back to the U.S. for burial. They will notify his family as well."

"I don't think he had any family," said Haden slowly, still stunned. Garza could see she was upset.

"It was our fault," he said. "We did not know she was so well armed and so dangerous. We had no idea she could shoot so well. If we did, we would have come with more force, been more careful. We thought it was just some woman wanted for crimes in your country."

"No, it was our fault. VanDerlies and I knew. We knew how dangerous she was. She already killed another FBI agent in New York and a lot of other people too. When I met her, I felt like I was in the presence of a monster. Do you think she is dead?"

"I am certain. We got her, you can rest assured."

Chapter Forty-Three
Dominical, Costa Rica

OIJ agent Gabriel Solano had seen death before. For two years he worked the meanest barrios of San Jose, first as a uniformed officer of the *Fuerza Publica* and later as an investigator for the OIJ. When he was transferred to the OIJ offices in Quepos with its rampant tourism and wealthy foreign residents, he did not expect to see many more dead bodies. But he had never seen anything like the scene in this Dominical villa. A total of twenty bodies lay in various positions of repose throughout the villa. The smell of blood and cordite permeated the air. Cartridges lay all over the front room, pool patio, kitchen and bedrooms.

Solano was told that the occupant of the villa was some Colombian drug lord. His bodyguards seemed well armed with AR-15 rifles and Glock pistols scattered on the ground. Saddest to Solano were the bodies of young women, eight in all and the kitchen workers and maids who had been slaughtered unarmed, cowering in terror.

A forensics team was scouring the villa for fingerprints, picking up brass cartridges to analyze for prints and attempting to find any other evidence of who was responsible. Solano speculated that there must have been more than one gunman. The wounds appeared to have been made by more than one weapon, an assault rifle of some sort and a pistol. He did not understand how the assailants got into the walled and heavily fortified villa. There was no sign of forced entry. Was it possible the killers were known to the villa occupants and let in voluntarily?

His fellow Quepos OIJ agent, Juan Garza, had been involved in a vicious firefight at the marina. He was assisting two American law enforcement visitors apprehending a fugitive wanted in the U.S.

That exercise cost the lives of two *Fuerza Publica* officers, one had just been reported as dying in hospital, and an FBI agent. The female homicide detective that accompanied them seemed to think that the suspect, a young woman suspected of murder in the U.S., could have been responsible for the massacre in Dominical. To Solano that seemed absurd. This was the work of hardened killers and it would take more than one little woman to do this kind of damage. Besides, Solano could not imagine any woman he ever knew being capable of slaughtering unarmed, innocent victims like the maids, kitchen workers and *putas* who had been brutally executed here. Even the cruelest woman was not capable of such viciousness. Besides there was not a scrap of evidence linking their suspect to this massacre.

Solano's best guess was that these were Colombian thugs from the same cartel as the villa's occupants who had been let in and then betrayed their comrades as part of an inter-cartel power struggle. That explained their gaining entry without forcing their way in and factored in the element of surprise that may have caught the victims off guard giving the assailants an advantage. Everyone knew these Colombian cartels were full of bloodthirsty monsters and this bloody mess was clearly the work of a bloodthirsty monster.

Chapter Forty-Four
Medellin, Colombia

Escalante and Bonilla were meeting almost every week lately to deal with the problems created by *Los Urbenos*. The Medellin Cartel was actually five smaller cartels that arose in the wake of the arrest of Pablo Escobar. Those five cartels had united in a loose federation. The five cartel leaders, of which Escalante was the most powerful, formed a kind of board of directors with Bonilla the sixth member. It took four votes to do most things. When it came to international, legal and banking issues it was always Bonilla who was directed to implement the decisions of the board

Today they were meeting in a small, elegant Medellin restaurant called Carmen. Bonilla said he would pay so Escalante opted for an expensive place with good food and an extensive bar menu. Of course, Escalante got there first. When Bonilla finally arrived and was shown to the table, he was ecstatic "I have very good news so I think we should celebrate with champagne," he said gesturing to the waiter.

"What news could be so good it warrants a bottle of overpriced champagne?"

"The death of Marcos Lucero. The demise of *Los Urbenos*."

"Are you certain?"

"The report out of Costa Rica is that Lucero and all his *sicarios* were found shot to death in his villa. The identity of his body has been confirmed. Lucero had no succession plan. He believed that grooming a next in command was grooming your own future murderer. The next level down from him are just foot soldiers incapable of taking control of the organization. We have just eliminated a competitor."

"I suppose this was the work of your hand-picked assassin?"

"You can be assured," nodded Bonilla as the waiter poured them glasses of bubbly straw-colored liquid in crystal flutes. "He accepted our down payment and indicated he would do the job which is now done. Admit it, you thought it was foolhardy to shell out so much money in advance for such a difficult job. Do you doubt now that our half million was well spent?"

"No, in retrospect it would have been worth even more to take *Los Urbenos* off the playing field. It will mean millions in increased sales to lose our biggest competitor."

"I will wire the remaining three hundred and fifty thousand to our man as soon as I get back to my office. He's probably not someone you would want to cross. Besides we will want his services in the future. There always seems to be someone who needs to be murdered in this business."

"Well, now that our greatest competitor is gone, I wonder where we need to go from here," mused Escalante.

"First, we must take down the labs *Los Urbenos* runs while they are in a state of chaos. We need to call a meeting of *El Seis* to authorize action. We can put together teams for that and to take down their distribution point in Buenaventura. I suggest we meet on Friday so we may act quickly."

Escalante nodded his agreement. He thought that Bonilla was increasingly acting as the leader of the Medellin Cartel instead of its chief counselor. He knew Bonilla was smart and ruthless but he was not an actual member of any cartel, not from Medellin, not from the same social class as the leaders of the five member cartels. They had all grown up in the drug dealing business. Some even worked with Escobar in the halcyon days of the great cartel that started it all. Bonilla came from an upper-class Bogota family, was educated in the United States. He belonged to all the right clubs and groups and hobnobbed with members of the national legislature. As he sipped his champagne, Escalante reflected that Bonilla was not the right person to be the leader of the unified Medellin cartels. *He is not one of us and he will not be our leader.*

Chapter Forty-Five
Spackenkill Hamlet, New York State

Haden felt obligated to attend VanDerlies' funeral. It was not that she felt responsible for his death, exactly, but she did feel as if she could have more strongly warned him about the dangerousness of the woman they were pursuing. For whatever reason, overconfidence, sexism, foolhardiness, VanDerlies never accepted the fact that they were chasing a monster, one who was every bit as dangerous as any horror film fiend. She felt that even before her face-to-face encounter with the woman and even more so after actually being in her presence. The woman's beauty and calm, casual manner were a camouflage for an intense savagery rarely encountered in any human of either sex fueled by a fierce intelligence.

When Haden heard about the Dominical massacre, she understood why the woman had been in Costa Rica. The primary victim was a high-ranking Colombian cartel leader. What she and VanDerlies had not known was that the woman was working in some capacity for a rival Colombian cartel. It would be unusual for the Colombians to employ an American and even more unusual for them to employ a woman. The Costa Rican authorities were sure that she had nothing to do with the massacre. They speculated that perhaps the rival cartel landed a task force of assassins by boat who somehow managed to take the villa occupants by surprise. Haden knew who actually did it.

The drive upstate to Spackenkill Hamlet, where the VanDerlies burial plot was located, was long and slow. The further she got from New York City the smaller and more rural the towns she passed through. Finally, her GPS guided her to a small, very old, graveyard between a corn field and a cow pasture. The wrought iron gates were rusty and hanging askew from the iron fence surrounding the plots. The graveyard looked neglected. Weeds grew everywhere, the trees were old and gnarled. No one had raked leaves in weeks. Haden got there as the hearse was pulling up to the grave site. She was shocked that there was no one else but the mortuary attendants and a middle-aged woman. Haden parked her car and walked to the grave site. The older woman turned to her and offered a hand. "Patricia Patterson, FBI," she said.

"Becky Haden, NYPD."

"I know who you are. You worked with Chandler Diaz then with VanDerlies on this case."

"I felt I had to come. In a sense we were partners and I was there when he was killed. I'm not sure I liked him much but I feel terrible about what happened. I can't believe we're the only ones here."

"VanDerlies was not very popular. He was a good agent but a terrible team player and he made a lot of enemies. I doubt anyone he worked with would have bothered to come."

"Why did you come?"

"I recruited him for this assignment. So, in a way I feel responsible for what happened to him. I thought I was doing him a favor by bringing him back on. I believed he could track Diaz' killer down. Well, I guess he did, but we may have underestimated how dangerous this killer is."

She paused for a moment as the mortuary attendants unloaded VanDerlies' coffin from the hearse and rolled it on its carrier toward the hole in the ground.

"I think I knew, or at least guessed, that this woman was lethally dangerous," said Haden as she watched the coffin lowered into the ground on slings. "It's one reason I feel so guilty. I knew we were being led into a trap and I just let VanDerlies take the lead. He was so sure of himself."

"You actually came face to face with her, didn't you?"

"Yes. It was clear she knew who I was and what I was doing in Quepos. I have to admit she terrified me. In her presence I felt a chill as if I were next to some sort of lethal monster."

"The Costa Rican authorities seem to think she is dead," said Patterson.

"I hope so but they never found a body, did they?"

"No, Costa Rican authorities said they swept the bottom of the marina but found nothing. They think the body was swept out to sea." Patterson paused to allow the minister to say a few words before the grave was covered over. They were still the only two onlookers. "They also don't believe our girl was responsible for that massacre in Dominical. At this point we may as well assume she is dead until we have evidence to the contrary. You and VanDerlies did a very good job tracking her down. I have to say that both Agent Diaz and VanDerlies were very complimentary about your competency. Diaz insisted he be allowed to work with you on the New York killings. For VanDerlies to compliment anyone, especially a woman, you know he was deeply misogynistic, was highly unusual. He spoke very highly of your abilities."

"I just wish he'd listened to me more. I wish I had warned him more clearly about the possibility of a trap. If I had maybe he would be alive today."

"You can't speculate about that. He was the lead agent and you followed his direction. If he led you into a trap, so be it. It doesn't sound as if our lady assassin came out of the fire fight any better off than VanDerlies. Look, I would be interested in having you apply with the Agency. I think you would be a wonderful agent and we need more women. Would you consider it?"

"Don't agents have to have special qualifications like law degrees or something?"

"There are exceptions. With your background I don't think you would have a problem. We would be happy to have you."

Haden smiled at her and took her hand.

"Thank you," she said. "Right now, I'm a little traumatized. I would be interested. Thank you for your offer."

They nodded to each other and walked off to their respective cars.

Chapter Forty-Six
NYPD Headquarters, New York City

It was three weeks after VanDerlies' funeral. She had been given leave due to the trauma of seeing her partner murdered in front of her. She took advantage of the time to terminate her pregnancy. She told herself that VanDerlies' death made it necessary to terminate since he would not be there to support them emotionally or financially. She knew this to be a lie she told herself. She never planned to tell him about the pregnancy. She only blurted it out from anger. As for emotional or financial support, that was a joke. VanDerlies had no money and was incapable of any kind of emotional support to anyone. If she were honest with herself, she would admit that she was unfit and unready to be a mother now and selfishly wanted to advance her career without a tiny impediment.

Now, back at her desk in homicide she found a pile of files in her inbox. At the very top was a report from the Costa Rican OIJ on the shootings at the Quepos Marina. Underneath that was a report on the massacre at a villa in Dominical which occurred shortly before the Quepos Marina action.

In the first report the OIJ detailed the request by the FBI, through the United States' embassy, to arrest a woman going under the name Amy Zyler. OIJ received a communication from the FBI that a rental boat had been reserved in the name of Amy Zyler to be picked up at the Quepos Marina. OIJ had its local agent notify VanDerlies and Haden to assist in the arrest. The report noted that the Zyler woman had committed no crimes in Costa Rica and was being detained at the request of United States' authorities. The report noted that these same U.S. authorities failed to notify OIJ that the subject was armed and dangerous.

Haden was sure that was untrue. She remembered discussing with Juan Garza the fact that the woman was suspected of multiple killings some of which had been quite vicious. They had no way to know that she was armed. In fact, the report indicated that the cartridges they found on the boat the suspect fired from were from an AR-15 which could not be traced. OIJ had no idea where or how she had obtained the weapon. The rifle itself could not be found. The report noted that fire from the boat initially caught the arresting officers off guard and there were three casualties. Two uniformed *Fuerza Publica* officers were hit, one dying at the scene the other after being transported to hospital. The third casualty was FBI agent Eric VanDerlies who accompanied the arresting team, was not armed or authorized to make an arrest. VanDerlies, too, was hit almost immediately and died at the scene.

The remaining officers returned fire and were joined by an additional three *Fuerza Publica* uniformed officers. Eventually, it appeared the suspect was hit and fell into the water. The arrest team waited a safe interval to approach the boat and found it empty. A large pool of blood, which was found to be A positive, was on the deck of the boat. Later lab analysis failed to identify a DNA match for the blood. No body or weapons were found on board although there were numerous cartridge shells which proved to be from an AR-15. Maritime authorities conducted a sweep of the marina to find the body and weapon but were unsuccessful. The report concluded, as Patterson told her, that the suspect was killed and her body swept away by prevailing currents along with the weapon she used. No personal effects of any kind were found on the boat.

The second report contained a number of photographs, which even in black and white, were quite grisly. The villa had been rented by a Panamanian corporation of unknown ownership. Among the dead were Marcos Lucero, a Colombian known to be the head of a drug smuggling organization called *Los Urbenos* based on the Pacific coast of Colombia and derived from a right-wing militia force which, prior to the recent armistice, fought the Marxist FARC guerillas. Also found were the bodies of six individuals identified by Colombian authorities as members of *Los Urbenos*. The report presumed they were bodyguards for Lucero. Eight young women were found dead. Four on the pool patio and four in the front sitting room. The ones in the sitting room had been raked with automatic weapons fire. The ones by the pool had been hit with automatic fire and finished off with bullets to the head. They were identified as prostitutes working out of the town of Jaco.

Also found dead were three kitchen workers, shot through the head. Two maids were found, similarly shot execution style in upstairs closets. Three of the bodyguards were shot with a nine-millimeter Beretta pistol. The remaining casualties were hit with AR-15 fire. A number of weapons were found in the villa, military models of the AR-15 and Glock pistols, along with large amounts of ammunition. Empty cartridge shells were found throughout the house but the only fingerprints to be found were those of the villa occupants. Nor could any other prints be found anywhere in the villa.

The OIJ speculated that a fire team from Panama landed on one of the local beaches. It was possible that a plant in the villa let them in and assisted them in surprising Lucero and his men. The sponsor of the raid was clearly a rival cartel seeking to snuff out competition.

Haden spent several hours going over the reports. She was bothered by the conclusions the OIJ drew. She should have been happy that they thought the woman was dead. As Patterson said, VanDerlies' death was not entirely in vain if a monster was removed from the earth. Something bothered her about the scenario laid out in the reports.

She felt sure that the Dominical massacre was the work of their subject. Law enforcement was always underestimating this woman and the OIJ did it again. It seemed unlikely that a single woman could have defeated seven well-armed, seasoned thugs. This woman was very smart and could have found a way to insinuate herself into the villa and used the element of surprise to get the drop on the hard partying Colombians.

As for the marina action, the whole situation seemed questionable to Haden. The woman knew they were there and that they were after her. If she had not known her Amy Zyler identity had been blown before, she must have known it when the FBI showed up at the very hotel for which she made reservations. So why use the name again? It was certain to alert them to her whereabouts and means of escape.

Haden suddenly had an idea. She desperately hoped she was wrong but she had to know. She went to her computer and used a law enforcement authorization to access Southern California birth records twenty-seven years before, hoping the data had been digitalized. She searched the name Ariella Blumkin. She got a hit. A seven-pound three-ounce baby girl had been born in Torrance Memorial hospital to Arkedy and Liana Blumkin. It was noted that Arkedy was deceased at the time of birth. Haden scrolled down to the health information and was horrified to finally find what she wanted. Baby Ariella Blumkin had an O negative blood type.

Also by the Author
at
Rogue Phoenix Press

Curse of Ciudad Blanca

Peter VanOwen is living by the beach in Costa Rica when his old college roommate, a disgraced professor of archaeology, drops in unexpectedly to convince him to go on an expedition to discover a lost city in the Honduran jungle and help resurrect his career. He is enticed to join the expedition by the prospect of seeing once again his long-lost college girlfriend who has remained the love of his life. But once in Honduras he encounters a sinister and mysterious woman who entraps him into going on an expedition he had intended to avoid. Upon penetrating deep into the Honduran jungle in search of the lost city VanOwen comes face to face with a sinister reality that will change his life and that of his family, friends and even his ex-girlfriend.

One
PLAYA ESTERILLOS, COSTA RICA

The rainy season always made his joints ache. Almost every afternoon the clouds gathered over Playa Esterillos, slowly darkening until the sky exploded with thunder, lightning and rain often lasting all night. Peter loved the pounding rain on the tin roof of his roasting shed and the acrid smell of roasting coffee over the humid air.

When he was not visiting coffee growers in the central highlands, he followed the same routine each day. In the warm, dry mornings he stepped out of his compound onto the empty, grey sand beach. He would bring a thermal pot of coffee and lie on his chaise longue reading from his Kindle. Occasionally he entered the warm, calm water. By eleven AM he left the beach to fix a light lunch and check his computer for e-mails. In the afternoon as the humidity rose and the clouds gathered, he would retreat to his roasting shed to sample and experiment with the coffee beans he was considering recommending to his clients in the U.S.

The current batch of beans was from the area around San Vito, a town settled in the nineteen-fifties by Italian immigrants in the southern mountains of central Costa Rica. The beans were plump with promise: smooth and blue-green. His challenge was to find the ideal roast by roasting small batches to various levels, experimenting with temperature and duration. In his shed, he had a small one-kilo Diedrich sample roaster powered by propane. Peter spent his afternoons in the shed roasting batch after batch, sampling the results and recording his findings. He loved the smell, texture and sound of the beans as they progressed through the roasting process.

For Peter, coffee roasting was an escape. Immersion in the process let him lose himself in something outside himself. The deep calm he felt as he processed each batch was the result of escaping his own consciousness and savoring the details of the roast. When the results were good, when he had extracted the ideal balance between body and flavor for the particular bean, he felt a deep sense of satisfaction and accomplishment unconnected with the objective importance of well roasted coffee.

In an earlier life, Peter VanOwen had been a lawyer employed by the Los Angeles County Counsel's office. For a while he had a wife and children and a small house in a Los Angeles suburb. A rancorous divorce and early retirement led him to Costa Rica and a stucco house in a gated compound on the grey volcanic beach of Playa Esterillos on the Pacific coast. He had stumbled into coffee brokering more as a way to fill his days than a need to make money. But he had come to love the process and discovered in himself an entrepreneurial side which had lain dormant over his years as a public lawyer. He bought coffee from small growers and sold it to several modest-sized coffee shop chains in the United States with recommendations on the roast and brewing. He often travelled throughout the central Costa Rican highlands looking for beans and occasionally travelled to Guatemala and Panama. Several times a month he would drive to San José to meet buyers. In between trips, he settled into his comfortable daily routine, seldom communicating with any of his old family and friends in California. His simple, isolated life suited him and he rarely felt a moment of loneliness. He loved the tropical weather, green, lush foliage and the easy, unhurried pace of Costa Rica.

Playa Esterillos had its share of American émigrés but Peter avoided them, as well as the nearby surfer town of Jaco with its high-rise hotels, surf shops and fish taco joints. He drank at home, not wanting to engage in the banal and self-promoting conversation of the typical American bar in Costa Rica. At 60 he had, he admitted to himself, become withdrawn and introspective.

As he watched the temperature on the Diedrich, Peter heard a car pull into his drive. He walked to the shed window to see a hired van expel a slight man with dark rimmed-glasses and ginger-colored hair, a man whom Peter had not seen for many years.

Other Books by the Author
at
Rogue Phoenix Press

Black Orchid

FBI Agent Chandler Diaz was assigned to investigate a string of well executed and brutal homicides in places as far flung as Singapore, Honduras and New York City. Even an investigator as talented as Diaz is having problems solving these crimes. Meanwhile, in Los Angeles, young lawyer, Fred Cornwall, notoriously unsuccessful with the opposite sex, thought he met the girl of his dreams in a kitschy Chinatown bar. She is smart, beautiful and has a lot of secrets. She wines and dines him and dazzles him with her beauty and wealth. But when he starts to learn some of her secrets, and a secret about himself, the dream starts to unravel.

The Other Side of Paradise

Aaron Jenks left his surgical practice in Los Angeles along with his wife and two daughters after a nasty divorce to retire to Costa Rica. A chance encounter in a posh Escazu café leads Aaron to the beautiful Nicole L'Heureaux, wife of the head of an old and prominent family whose history parallels the darkest aspects of the history of the Central American nation. Nicole is bored, ambitious and ruthless, unhappy in her marriage and contemptuous of her husband and his family. .Aaron's passion for Nicole leads him to radically change his life and the lives of his daughter and girlfriend in unexpected ways. For Aaron his pursuit of Nicole leads down a dark and desperate path. Costa Rica is a place of great natural beauty but where human passion and greed are involved there is another side to paradise.

About the Author

Robert V Wadden Jr. is a retired attorney splitting his time between his homes in the Los Angeles area and Esterillos, Costa Rica.

VISIT OUR WEBSITE

FOR THE FULL INVENTORY

OF QUALITY BOOKS:
http://www.roguephoenixpress.com

Rogue Phoenix Press
Representing Excellence in Publishing

Quality trade paperbacks and downloads

in multiple formats,

in genres ranging from historical to contemporary romance, mystery and science fiction.

Visit the website then bookmark it.

We add new titles each month!